THE STON
MYSTERIES

-1-

THE CURIOUS DISPATCH OF
DANIEL COSTELLO

CHRIS MCDONALD

RED DOG
UK

Published by RED DOG PRESS 2021

First Edition

Paperback ISBN 978-1-913331-87-0

Ebook ISBN 978-1-913331-88-7

www.reddogpress.co.uk

1

A NIGHT TO FORGET

THE POUNDING DANCE music and the pulsing lights were everything Sam had hoped for and more. He'd loved this type of music since his teens and had set his heart on coming to Ibiza for his stag do ever since he'd first heard the opening notes to Adagio for Strings more than a decade ago.

Now that he was here, everything seemed... amplified; bigger than he'd imagined it. The music was louder, the beer was cheaper, and the girls were even more scantily dressed than he'd ever dared to envisage.

Of course, he was here on his stag, but a man could window shop, couldn't he?

He waved his hands in the air as the beat dropped and, along with the mass of bodies around him, writhed in time with the thumping bass. He took a swig from his bottle of beer, spilling some down the front of his custom-made T-shirt – a pink monstrosity with a horned stag front and centre, Sam's smiling face photoshopped in the middle of it all. He'd been forced into it at the airport and the boys had made enough of them to make sure he wore nothing else all week.

He looked around the bustling club, scanning for any of his mates, but everyone seemed to have either scattered or called it a night completely. He didn't have a watch, and the windowless room gave no clue as to what time it might be. He thought about having one last drink, but the tiredness tugged at his eyelids, exacerbated by the unholy amount of alcohol he'd consumed. The only thing keeping him going was that pill he'd taken.

As he made to leave the dancefloor, a hand reached out, the fingers interlocking with his own, pulling him back.

A pretty brunette swam into view. Her features weren't unlike Emily's, his future wife's, though her eyes were slightly bigger. She leaned in close to him, affording Sam a sneaky peak at her cleavage as her top gaped.

'Leaving so soon?' she shouted in his ear, above the swell of the music.

She pulled back, and he stared at her with bleary eyes, trying to make sense of what she was saying. Once it had computed, he nodded.

'One more dance,' she mouthed, leading him back to the middle of the dancefloor. He followed her, taking in her short skirt and tanned, shapely legs. When she reached the desired spot, she turned, and they danced, getting progressively closer until their noses were almost touching.

'I'm getting married,' he slurred, as he looked into her dark eyes.

'Me too,' she replied, holding up her hand to show a diamond encrusted ring. 'Everyone gets a freebie on their hen do, though.'

She took one more step and brushed her lips against his. He thought about pulling away, but only for a moment. Instead, he moved closer and pressed his lips firmly onto hers. Images of Emily swam through his drunken thoughts and this time he did pull away, mumbling his apologies. She shrugged, turned, and having got what she wanted, disappeared into the crowd.

Tears formed in the corner of his eyes and his cheeks burned with the shame of what he'd just done.

Looking up, Sam locked eyes with Danny. He wondered how much his best man had seen. Aside from the flashing lights, the place was dark and full of revellers – surely, he couldn't have seen the whole show. As Sam left the dancefloor and approached him, the answer was clear. Danny was looking at him with raised eyebrows and a slight grin.

'You dirty dog,' he said, clapping him on the shoulder as they exited the club.

Sam looked at him with a plea in his eyes.

'It was a mistake. She kissed me,' he murmured. 'You can't tell anyone.'

Danny held up a placating hand and dragged a finger across his chest, sketching an X.

'Don't worry, big man. I'll take it to the grave.'

ONE MONTH LATER

2

AN UNFORTUNATE INSIGHT INTO THE LIFE OF ADAM WHYTE

ADAM WHYTE SLIPPED a hand into his pyjama bottoms and scratched his undercarriage for quite an extended period of time. When his hand emerged, he lifted it to his nose and gave it a sniff. Though the smell was not pleasant, his face didn't show any displeasure. On the contrary. He judged the smell to be just the right side of acceptable and decided to push back his probably much-needed shower until tomorrow. His mum had been watching all of this happen from behind a book, a look of disgust etched on her face.

Adam lifted a pint glass full of water from the ground and slurped from it, before grabbing the PlayStation controller and expertly navigating through the home page of Netflix. He tapped a few buttons and the theme song for Sherlock began.

'Oh, haven't you watched enough of this today?' his mum asked.

'You can never get enough of the Cumberbatch, can you?' Adam replied.

She sighed and thought about her son. From an early age, he'd pretended to be a 'sloof', solving make-believe crimes with his friends. A few years ago, he had travelled sixty miles up the road to Belfast, to study psychology at Queens University. Predictably, he hadn't lasted long. In true Adam Whyte fashion, he'd become the popular lad on campus, much to the detriment of his studies. And so, after less than a year, he'd returned home, to the north coast of Northern Ireland; to Stonebridge, and had been stuck in dead end jobs since. Until a few days ago, that was, when he'd been fired from the pub he was working in, due to being late one too many times. Gone were the dreams of joining the police; of becoming a detective. Now, here he was, unapologetically scratching his balls in the middle of the afternoon in front of his own mother.

She watched him cover his eyes as the detective on the screen surveyed a blood-soaked body. Adam had never been good with blood – another reason a career in the police was never going to happen.

'Are you looking forward to the wedding tomorrow?' she asked him.

'It'll be good to see friends, yeah,' he said. 'And it's tradition for the groomsman to snog a bridesmaid, so there's that.'

He raised his eyebrows suggestively before turning back to the TV.

I wouldn't hold out much hope, she thought to herself, turning her attention back to her book.

3

A MIX UP

ADAM'S BATTERED RENAULT Clio crawled along the wide gravel driveway that was framed by sprawling, manicured lawns. Tall oak trees and Victorian lampposts alternated alongside the path.

Adam thought that if the ancient trees could talk, they'd probably tell him that his car was the worst vehicle they'd ever seen and that it simply being on the property was enough to tarnish the land.

After cresting a small hill, the stately home loomed in front of them. Tamed ivy crept tastefully across the stone walls and beautifully crafted statues of lions kept guard on either side of a huge, wooden door. The clifftop property, framed by the endless ocean behind it, was a stunning place for a marriage.

'Hard to believe we're only thirty minutes from home,' Adam said. 'Feels like we're in the middle of nowhere.'

He entered the car park and found a space. Colin, Adam's best friend, got out of the car and looked around. He stretched his lanky frame and looked to the unbroken blue sky.

'What's hard to believe is that they booked their wedding on the Twelfth weekend, of all the weekends available,' he said. 'I'm supposed to be getting smashed and watching some marching bands.'

'Oh, Colin,' Adam said, clapping his friend on the shoulder and pushing him towards the door. 'So uncultured. This is going to be so much better. There's going to be no drama, for one, and everyone knows girls let their inhibitions go at weddings. You might even get lucky!'

They walked in the front door and set their bags down, taking in their surroundings. Original wooden floorboards were paired tastefully with dark stone walls upon which framed portraits hung. A wide chandelier dangled above their heads, the golden sunlight that flowed in through a large window catching in the crystal fixtures. They followed the strip of red carpet that led from the door to the unmanned reception desk. They rang the bell and a second later, a well-groomed, suited man greeted them with a wide smile and a warm hello.

'We've got two rooms, under Whyte and McLaughlin,' Adam told him.

The man, his nametag announcing him as Francis, manoeuvred the mouse and clicked a few buttons on the computer, though a frown spread across his face and he started to shake his head slowly.

'We've got *a* room for Whyte and McLaughlin.'

Adam looked up at Colin, who appeared suitably confused. Realisation dawned slowly on his face and he squeezed his eyes shut.

'You've messed the booking up, haven't you?' he said to his friend, shaking his head. It was like their trip to London all over again.

He turned back to Francis, not waiting for an answer.

'Do you have any other rooms available?'

'No, I'm sorry,' Francis replied, shaking his head. 'All the rooms have been booked months in advance, due to the wedding.'

'Great,' Adam said sarcastically, taking the proffered key for their shared room. Francis told them that if anyone cancelled, they'd be the first to know.

Adam lambasted Colin all the way up the stairs. They turned left at the top of the steps and began making their way towards room number 14, stopping by a bay window to take in the sea view. The sun shimmered on the water below and they watched the waves break on the cliffs, the white spray splashing high into the air. As a seagull swooped and rose high into the sky again, they tore themselves away from the view and found their room at the end of the corridor. Adam turned the key in the lock and pushed the door open, revealing a beautifully decorated room.

A desk sat alongside one wall, a notepad and a pen perched on top. Various framed pieces of art decorated the recently painted cream walls, and a bookcase in the corner of the room held a selection of weighty classics. As nice as it was, there was one big problem.

Pushed against one of the walls was one double bed.

'You've got to be kidding me,' Adam mumbled.

SLEEPING ARRANGEMENTS DECIDED, (top and tail – not ideal but a compromise all the same) Adam and Colin set about getting ready for the first night of drinking. Adam pulled on his favourite pair of chinos – navy – and a red and black flannel shirt. He spread wax through his dark hair, trying to achieve the *just out of bed* look. He briefly considered shaving his slightly patchy beard, but he'd been growing it for a couple of weeks now and couldn't bear to part with it.

He looked across at Colin, who had settled on casual jeans and a white T-shirt, and felt the jealousy rise as he considered his friend's fulsome facial hair. Some people have all the luck.

Since primary school, he and Colin had been inseparable. As puberty had struck, the changes had set in. Colin had grown to six foot and developed wide shoulders which were used to good effect on the school's rugby team. Adam stayed at just over five and a half feet, and his weedy appearance had caused him to be picked last for any sport. They were nicknamed Little and Large, for obvious reasons.

Once ready, Adam pulled a DVD player from his bag and set about connecting it to the small TV already in the room. Colin gave him a questioning look.

'I thought we'd have a bit of spare time this weekend. The wedding isn't until Sunday, that leaves us with a lot of free time tomorrow. I thought we'd work our way through this,' he said, holding up series one of Sherlock.

'Great shout,' Colin answered, as his friend slipped disk one into the tray.

The next hour and a half passed quickly, both of them lost in an episode they had watched countless times.

'I have to go to this rehearsal thing,' Adam said, checking his watch as the credits rolled. 'It shouldn't take too long and then I'll meet you in the bar?'

'No worries,' replied Colin, taking a book out of his bag and settling down on the bed. Before he could open the book, his attention was quickly drawn away as he watched Adam make some last-minute changes to his hair. He shook his head at his friend's vanity.

'I can't believe I'm having to spend the weekend with bloody Daniel Costello,' he said.

'I know,' Adam replied. 'Odd choice for Best Man. I assumed his twin would've been nailed on for that job, but then, Danny and Sam were always close. The speech is going to be a train wreck, I reckon.'

With that, he headed for the door.

'Are you not taking your phone?' Colin shouted after him, holding up the iPhone that had been lying on the bed next to him.

'No point, there's barely any reception.'

He bid Colin a swift goodbye and walked down the corridor to Sam's room – the bridal suite. The groom-to-be's face lit up when he opened the door and saw who was behind it. He ushered Adam into the huge room, complete with king sized four poster bed and a glorious sea view.

Adam looked Sam up and down. He'd lost quite a bit of weight in the couple of weeks since they'd last hung out – presumably the work of the personal trainer he'd paid handsomely. Adam made a mental note to ask for his name.

'Alright, mate,' said Danny, who was sprawled on the bed. His shirt was buttoned down to near his bellybutton and he carried with him that sense of arrogance he always had, though had done nothing to earn.

'I'm good thanks,' Adam replied. He'd never had much time for Danny. He turned to Ross, Sam's twin. 'How you doing, man?'

Ross stood up and shook his hand, a wide grin on his face. Like Sam, Ross had thick, dark hair and gangly features. It had been nigh on impossible to tell them apart through school, though was slightly easier now on account of Ross's mangled accent – Northern Irish with a hint of Lancashire – which he had acquired from having spent four years at university in Lancaster. He was probably the only person in the whole country who supported Preston North End, too.

'Where's Emily?' Adam asked Sam.

'She's at her parent's place. Her side of the family are coming tomorrow evening for the meal. Until then, it's just us.'

'A bit like Lord of the Flies. A load of reprobates let loose in a house,' sniggered Danny.

Adam was pretty sure that Danny had never read that particular book. Come to think of it, he wasn't sure if Danny could read at all. Again, he ignored Danny's comment and addressed Sam.

'Sorry I couldn't make the stag; money is a bit tight at the moment and mum had already offered to pay for this weekend so I couldn't scrounge any more off her. It looked like you all had a great time.'

'It was a lot of fun,' Danny laughed. 'Sam had a great time, didn't you?'

A flash of *something* passed over Sam's features. Anger? When he spoke, though, his tone was nonchalant.

'Yeah, it was great, thanks. I tried paella for the first time, and we hired jet skis and mucked about in the bay. The nights out were mad, too. I've not drank since!'

Danny looked like he was about to add something, but was cut off by Sam pulling out a box from under the bed. From it, he produced four silver hipflasks and handed one to Ross, Danny and Adam.

Adam inspected it. It felt heavy in his hand, and the engraved initials were a nice touch.

'It's filled with a ten-year-old Bushmills single malt, so cherish it,' Sam said. They each undid the tops, clinked the flasks together and took a hearty swig. It burned as it trickled down

Adam's throat and he did the same as the others; tried not to let the discomfort show.

'Let's get this rehearsal over with,' Sam said. 'Then the fun can begin.'

4

THE REHEARSAL

ADAM, SAM, ROSS and Danny walked down the stairs and out of the front door, breathing in the salty seaside air. They trooped across the grass and rounded the corner of the attractive house. Danny let out a long, impressed whistle at what he saw.

A huge white marquee sat in the middle of a wide garden, framed by the cloudless blue sky and a garden of roses that overlooked the sea.

They walked in through the open doors and took in the opulence. Rows of chairs, draped in ivory material and backed with a purple bow, filled the space. A wide aisle bisected them; the red carpet so thick it looked like you could sink into it. Fairy lights had been threaded through the material in the ceiling and five-feet-tall letters, spelling LOVE, had been positioned beside the stand-in alter at the front.

'Mate, this wedding must be costing you a fortune!' Danny laughed. 'Oh no, wait, it's not costing you a thing because you're marrying into North Coast royalty.'

The Campbell family, that Sam was marrying into, were well known for being high rollers. Emily's father, Trevor, was a stern man, as the CEO of a company probably had to be. He had a huge face, barely any neck, and the body shape of a gorilla. Her mother worked in one of the big banks in Belfast, only coming home at the weekends to their mansion by the sea in Stonebridge.

Trevor doted on his only daughter – it was the only thing he was ever soft about - and had offered to pay for the whole thing. He'd pulled strings and called in many a favour to get the weekend booked out at Milton Manor; the most exclusive venue in the area.

He was not a man to be trifled with.

The boys walked around the interior of the marquee, taking in the finer details and the stunning view from the large window. Adam watched Sam cast an admiring glance around, noticing the emotion in his eyes. This probably made everything seem a bit more real now.

They were interrupted by the arrival of the vicar, who shouted a cheery hello to get the boys' attention.

Reverend Fred, as they called him, was a well-known figure in their hometown and one of the nicest men in the world. As well as his weekly sermons, which none of the boys attended anymore, he was always at the heart of the community. Every Christmas, he took part in a sponsored sleep out, with all the money going to charity. He was often to be found in the shadow of the town hall, wrapped up in warm clothes and smiling at the late-night shoppers.

He called them to the front and they dutifully assembled, shaking his extended hand one at a time.

'Sam,' he said, turning to the front and smiling at the soon-to-be married man. 'I cannot believe that little Sammy who used to cry when his mummy dropped him off to Sunday school all those years ago is getting married.'

Fred winked at the rest of the boys, who pushed and jostled Sam playfully.

'I won't keep you for long, boys,' said Fred. 'I know you've got other things to attend to.'

For a few minutes, they listened intently to what Fred had to say. As the male contingent of the wedding party, their job was fairly simple. They'd all be at the front already, awaiting the arrival of the bride. The only thing anyone really had to do was Danny, who would be in charge of handing over the rings at the right time.

Fred then positioned them into roughly where they'd be standing. Sam in the centre, flanked by Danny, then Ross, with Adam at the end. When walking out, they'd pair up with a bridesmaid, link arms and make their way down the aisle and outside for photographs.

'Can one of you assume the role of Emily?' Fred asked. 'Just so that we can go through the vows. Sometimes it helps to say them once so that you know what's coming on the day.'

Danny stepped forward into the spot that Emily would be occupying on the actual day.

'Now, it'll have to be a secret that I'm marrying you two tonight,' Fred laughed. 'Don't tell Emily.'

'I'll add it to my ever-growing list of secrets,' Danny said, winking at Sam.

Only Sam seemed to know what Danny was talking about, judging by the colour of his face as he fought to bite back the rage.

The vicar carried on with the practice vows. Sam's voice caught on certain lines, and even Adam felt a little lump in his throat as he imagined how his friend was feeling.

After the vows, Sam and Fred hugged, before the vicar bid them goodbye. They watched him walk across the grass towards the car park.

'Let's go get smashed,' Danny said, breaking the icy silence.

5

A RIGHT OLD KNEES UP

COLIN MADE HIS way down the curved staircase, holding on to the heavy wooden banister. Safety was paramount in his workplace – The Stonebridge Retirement Home – and he often found himself adhering to the same rules he imposed on the old folks that he cared for. He often got funny looks from the visiting relatives – he supposed it wasn't all that usual for a man in his mid-twenties to work in such a place – but he loved every second of it and hoped to work there for many years to come.

Before he'd started there, he'd often assumed that old folk's homes were a stepping stone away from heaven. He'd started working there at weekends, to earn a bit of money while he studied at university, but he soon fell in love with the place and the people. His perceptions of old people changed immediately. They were full of life and stories, and he couldn't get enough. Upon graduating, he had immediately applied for a full-time position and was lucky enough to be offered the job. He'd never looked back.

When he reached the bottom of the stairs, he made his way through the foyer towards the room where all the noise was coming from. He smoothed his hair and opened the door, the volume of the music immediately increasing.

The wood-panelled room was huge. Circular tables with plush, velvet chairs around them took up most of the floor space, though a section at the end of the room had been set up as a makeshift dancefloor. Colourful lights blinked and twirled in preparation for whoever was brave enough to take to the black and white tiled floor first.

Colin scanned the room and found Adam at the bar, waiting to be served. Colin's feet sunk into the thick, green carpet as he crossed the room and snuck up on his friend.

'Looks like I've arrived just in time,' he said as he reached Adam, making him jump. 'Pint of Harp, please, and I'll go find a seat.'

Colin strode across the room towards an empty table next to a wide, decorative fireplace with a coat of arms fixed to the wall above it. A few minutes later, Adam plonked two pints and a couple of packets of crisps onto the table, before settling into the spare seat. Colin thanked him and took a huge gulp of the lager, the fizz immediately getting him in the mood for a big night.

Adam, on the other hand, seemed subdued. He thought about his interactions with people he hadn't seen since school. Most had moved to Belfast and were part way into their career. Some had even climbed a few rungs on that ladder already. He felt embarrassed having to admit that he'd dropped out of university, been unable to hold down a job and that he was still living at home with his mum. At school, he'd achieved excellent results in his exams, but what the teachers had constantly told him had turned out to be correct so far – he wasn't good at applying himself.

He took a sip from his pint and vowed to make a change – this time next year he'd have a job and a place of his own. He just needed to figure out what his calling was, and sometimes that took time.

He remembered reading that Susan Boyle had been 47 when she auditioned on whatever talent show she'd gone on, and the guy who founded McDonald's didn't do it until he was 59. Some people simply came into their own a little later in life – like a fine wine.

After that comforting thought, he cheered up a bit.

They stayed at the table for a while, sipping from pints and watching the room fill up around them. They knew a lot of people from their school days, and Adam recognised some of the faces as university pals of Sam's.

Shortly after eight o'clock, platters of food arrived from the kitchen, carried by a team of smartly dressed waiters. They placed the silver trays on a long table covered in a tartan tablecloth. It didn't take long for the aromas to drift to Adam's side of the room, and only then did he realise how hungry he was. He and Colin joined the queue and before long they were eagerly scooping an assortment of food onto their plates.

As Adam squirted a generous helping of ketchup over the pile of chips on his plate, he caught sight of Sam and Danny, huddled in the corner of the room.

It looked like they were arguing.

Danny showed Sam something on his iPhone, causing Sam to push him on the shoulder. Someone asked Adam if he was finished with the tomato sauce, causing him to take his eyes off what was happening between the groom and his best man. When he looked back, Sam was sitting alone and there was no sign of Danny.

Adam quickly moved on from what he had seen as his thoughts turned towards the mountain of food on his plate. A plate which was almost sent flying as Mike, Emily's brother, stumbled into Adam's path.

'Sorry, man,' he mumbled, before moving out of Adam's way, towards the bar. Adam watched him stumble away and marvelled at how brave he was in his fashion choices – pale green skinny jeans and a cravat were not the usual fare for the twenty-something Northern Irishman. Adam secretly wished he had the balls to try it, though.

BY TEN O'CLOCK, the food had long since vanished and the serious matter of drinking was well under way.

The dancefloor was filled, mostly with women, their dresses illuminated by the rainbow lights, while the men sat around the perimeter of the room, nursing pints and discussing the soon-to-be-closed Premier League transfer window. Some of the braver menfolk were already making their moves on the dancefloor, trying and failing to impress their targets. It reminded Adam of a primary school disco. Or a David Attenborough documentary. He wasn't sure which was sadder. He took Colin's drink order and walked to the bar. Whilst waiting to be served, he tried to strike up a conversation with a girl he recognised when he had visited Sam at his university across the water. She was polite, though declined his offer of a drink.

Typical, he thought, as he watched her carefully manoeuvre her way through the maze of tables and into the arms of a white shirted man. Adam turned his attention away from the couple and back to the bar. He ordered two pints and stood waiting while they were poured.

Suddenly, at a table nestled in an alcove to the rear of the bar, an altercation arose. One moment, Sam, Danny and Ross were chatting quietly, when all of a sudden Sam rose and shoved his best man in the chest.

Danny toppled over the back of his seat and banged his head on the carpeted floor. He rose gingerly and stood snarling, arms outstretched like a boxer. He shouted something that Adam couldn't hear over the music.

Sam attempted to push himself out of his seat, but his twin forced him back down. Instead, Ross formed a wall between the two. He said something to Danny who threw his arms in the arm, turned and stormed past the bar. Adam watched him march out of the room without so much as a backward glance. Ross went to follow him, but Sam grabbed his arm and shook his head.

It happened in the blink of an eye. Adam glanced around the bar to see if anyone else had been witness to it, but was pretty sure he had been the sole onlooker.

Had the best man position just become available?

He grabbed his order from the bar and walked back to the table. He relayed what he had just seen to Colin, who listened carefully and dismissed it as a silly argument fuelled by wedding nerves and alcohol.

The rest of the night passed in a haze as lager turned into spirits and spirits turned into shots. At just after midnight, Adam and Colin stumbled up the stairs and unlocked their room after a few bumbling attempts. They both mumbled expletives as their bleary eyes focussed on the singular bed.

Adam fell asleep thinking that Colin's feet smelled of brie.

6

NO SHOW AT BREAKFAST

ADAM WOKE UP in stages, head fuzzy with a monstrous hangover that was just getting going. Even without moving, he felt the contents of his stomach swirl, putting him in two minds – lie still and hope for the best, or run to the bathroom in preparation. The last thing he wanted was to throw up all over the bed and be handed a hefty cleaning bill.

His arm brushed against something in the bed – someone! With his eyes closed, he tried to piece together the night before. He remembered being shot down by an array of girls, but his memories trailed off shortly after that third shot…

Gingerly, he opened one eye. The light flowing in through the insubstantial fabric curtain caused him to wince in pain. The sight that greeted him wasn't much better.

Colin's hairy back and bum crack was not the first sight he'd have chosen for his eyes to settle on first thing in the morning. It did little to alleviate the sick feeling in his stomach.

Bathroom it was.

Ten minutes later, he emerged from the bathroom feeling slightly better, though the taste left in his mouth was unholy. He looked at himself in the mirror and chuckled.

He looked worse than he felt. If that was even possible.

He sat down on the edge of the bed, his head a cloud of pain. He unzipped his bag and fished in the front pocket, his hand clamping round its intended target. From the dimpled foil packet, he pushed out two tablets and guzzled them down with a glass of tap water.

A few minutes later, Colin joined him in the land of the living. He stretched his long limbs, yawned widely and jumped out of bed.

'Morning,' Adam croaked.

'Morning. You feeling rough?'

'I feel like I've been hit by a car.'

Colin chuckled. His friend had always been melodramatic. And terrible at holding his drink. He watched as Adam crawled into a foetal position on the bed, eyes closed.

'I'm going for a run before breakfast, to clear the cobwebs.'

Adam's reply was merely a look of disgust.

'It'd do you the world of good,' Colin laughed. 'What are you going to do instead?'

'Pray for mercy and try not to die.'

COLIN HAD ALWAYS found that life's problems could be sorted out with a quick run. Working where he did, he encountered death on a regular basis. He considered himself stoic, but each passing affected him. The relationships he had with each of the old folk were so much more than professional. He grew to love them and each death rocked him. One of the old hands who worked there told him that running was a great way to help the head process what the heart couldn't.

So, he did.

And he found that it worked a treat.

Today, though, he was running for a different reason. He liked to explore places he'd never been before, and running was a great way to do it.

He jogged at a leisurely pace down the country lane, watching the sheep doze lazily in vast fields while the wind buffeted him from behind, giving him an injection of pace.

Glancing to the other side, he took in the endless sea and the waves peacefully approaching the shore of the beach in the distance.

Sometimes, he took for granted how beautiful his part of the world was. Days like today reminded him that he shouldn't.

After fifteen minutes, he came to a corner and stopped to catch his breath. He wished he'd had the foresight to bring some water, but he hadn't banked on the sun being so hot so early in the morning.

Scanning the road, he saw a petrol station not far away; the only building to be seen amongst the rolling fields, aside from Milton Manor.

He picked up the pace and reached the petrol station in no time at all. The young man behind the desk watched Colin walk to the fridge and seemed surprised to have custom so early. Colin placed a bottle of ice-cold water on the counter and took out his card to pay.

'We only take cash,' the attendant apologised, pointing to a small handwritten note stuck to the counter. He looked at Colin's sweaty clothes and clocked his annoyance. 'But you can just have it. On me.'

Colin's mood immediately brightened, and he promised that he'd bring the money on the next visit. He left the shop and downed the water before putting the empty bottle in the bin. He looked up at the roof covering the forecourt, which only had two pumps. It was a family-owned business. The Cox family who owned it must've encountered trouble before, as they'd installed two CCTV cameras, one pointing at the pumps with the other aimed at the narrow road that passed by it.

Reinvigorated, Colin ran all the way back to the wedding venue, keen for a shower before breakfast.

THE LEMONY SCENT of Colin's shower gel mingled with the smell of greasy bacon, causing Adam problems. He pushed his breakfast around the plate, not trusting his stomach to deal with the soda bread and potato farls that he would have ordinarily devoured.

He wasn't the only one feeling the effects of last night.

Most were still in bed, unable to pull themselves from below their duvets, hoping that a few extra hours in bed would see them through the worst of the hangover.

Some who had braved breakfast were copying Adam, raising a forkful of food to their mouths before setting it back down on the plate, stomachs roiling.

A select few, like Colin, were wolfing their food down. Adam looked at their emptying plates with longing.

Sam, the groom, looked over from his table and caught Adam's eye, calling him over with a flick of his finger.

'Have you seen Danny this morning?' he asked when Adam was beside him.

Adam shook his head.

'No worries,' said Sam. 'We were supposed to be having breakfast together. I'll go and see where he is.'

'I'll go, you stay and finish your breakfast. I can't stomach mine.'

'If you see Ross, tell him to hurry up and all. He drove home last night to sort something with his new girlfriend and I've not seen him reappear yet.'

Adam left the stench of the breakfast behind and walked to Danny's room, which was on the ground floor at the far end of the building. He thought to himself that Danny probably hadn't set an alarm, or, if he had, he'd simply hit the snooze buttons one too many times. That, or he might still be pissed off with Sam over whatever they were arguing about last night.

He passed a marble bust of some old dude who used to own the house and approached Danny's door. When he knocked, the door slipped out of its lock and swung open.

Inside, the room was dark. The curtains were more heavy duty than in Adam's room and were doing a good job of keeping the sun out. As Adam's eyes adjusted, he could make out a mound on the bed, tucked in under the duvet.

Adam called out his name a few times, but got no response. He walked to the end of the bed and shook Danny by the ankles, again getting nothing. The guy wasn't even stirring.

He walked back to the curtains and opened them, letting light flood the room.

With the room illuminated, Adam noticed that the room was a mess. A lamp was lying on the floor, its shade left at an odd angle, the plug upturned. His case was lying open, the contents strewn across the floor.

Danny had always been messy, Adam thought. He remembered a school trip to France, ten years ago. Their dorm room had stank worse than the smelly cheeses they had been pressurised into trying by overzealous teachers, mostly on account of Danny's poor personal hygiene.

Rounding the corner of the bed, Adam noticed the vomit on the mattress and on the floor.

Ignoring the putrid stench and the uneasy bubbling feeling in his own stomach, he pulled the duvet back.

Danny lay on his back, his dark hair plastered to his forehead. His face was ghostly white, save for the drops of dried sick on his chin. He was wearing the clothes from the night before, the top button of his shirt torn off.

Adam checked for a pulse, already sure of the outcome. Sure enough, he couldn't feel anything.

Danny Costello was dead.

7

THE GAMECHANGER

ADAM SAT ON the steps of the hotel, gulping in the fresh air, having just thrown up in a bush to the side of the entrance, narrowly missing the stone mane of the proud lion.

He'd never been good with anything squeamish. Once, he'd driven an ex-girlfriend to hospital whose appendix was about to burst. He reluctantly went with her into the treatment room and noticed too late as they inserted a needle into a vein in her arm. A single drop of blood fell and spread onto the bedsheet, blossoming like red petals. To his shame, he'd made his excuses and ran to the bathroom, throwing up on the tiled floor as soon as he'd got through the door.

The relationship didn't last long after that.

A drop of blood was one thing. A dead body was something new altogether.

Adam would never forget the glassy eyes or the translucent skin or the smell that TV shows never managed to capture accurately. No one ever threw up after discovering a body either.

He thought back to his actions, and, despite shivering at the thought, was quietly proud of himself. He'd made sure that Danny was definitely dead and had managed to hold it together until he had phoned the police. He'd taken control of a pretty messed up situation, and that counted for something.

COLIN SAT BY his friend's side, trying to console him.

He couldn't imagine finding a dead body, let alone the body of someone you considered a friend.

An annoying friend.

A friend most people had had some sort of altercation with at some stage, but a friend all the same.

This kind of thing didn't happen to people like them.

In the distance, he heard sirens. If Adam hadn't been the one to find the body, they both would have been excited to be in the midst of a real-life investigation. As it was, there was nothing to look forward to.

What was supposed to be a celebratory weekend where two friends joined together in matrimony had quickly turned to a nightmare. As well as the horror of a dead friend, it also meant that the wedding was probably off, causing Sam and Emily to be out of pocket to the tune of thousands.

Well, the Campbell family, but potato potato.

Colin shook his head at how unfair life could be.

ADAM LOOKED UP as the sirens grew closer. He could see them beyond the hedgerow, turning slowly into the hotel's sweeping driveway.

A police car emerged from the tree lined approach, gravel spitting from under the tyres as the brakes were applied. An ambulance followed close behind. They stopped close to the elaborate water fountain, the blue lights stopped flashing and two police officers emerged from the car who looked like they'd rather be elsewhere got out. Two paramedics followed suit, busying themselves in the back of the ambulance, gathering the necessary equipment.

Gravel crunched underfoot as they made their way across the front of the building, surveying the impressive building with minimum appreciation. One wore a short sleeved shirt with aviator sunglasses perched on his nose. He clearly thought he was too cool for school.

The other was ginger and hunched and look like he'd been bullied at school so had taken the job solely for the power it would bestow upon him. Adam quickly formed a dislike for both of them.

'We believe there's been a bit of bother, lads,' Sunglasses said with a smirk.

'My friend has died,' Adam replied.

'Shame,' Ginger said, though clearly, he couldn't care less.

'Why is there only two of you?' Adam asked. 'Shouldn't there be CSIs and the coroner?'

Both of the police officers laughed at him.

'You watch too much TV, son,' Sunglasses scoffed, walking past them and up the steps towards the foyer of the hotel. Ginger followed, as did the paramedics.

As soon as they were out of sight, Adam and Colin got up and walked around the back of the hotel. Since Danny's room was on the ground floor, they figured they could watch the police go about their business through the window, as long as they did it covertly.

They carefully took their positions, one on either side of the window. They heard the heavy door creak open inside and listened to the man from reception tell the police and paramedics that they were short staffed. Ginger excused him with a grunt and he left the room, slamming the door closed.

Colin stole a glance inside.

The two police officers stood with their backs to the window, observing the body, while the paramedics performed a series of checks. After a few minutes, they spoke, though their deep voices didn't carry quite so well and Colin had trouble understanding them.

Adam watched as the paramedics repacked their things and left the room while the police officers performed a cursory glance around the room and then made for the door again. He looked at his watch. They hadn't even been in the room for ten minutes.

As Danny's door closed, Adam and Colin sprinted to the front of the building and retook their places on the steps just as the ambulance was pulling away. A few minutes later, the police officers reappeared.

'We've just spoken to the fella who is getting married and he told us that you were the one who discovered the body,' Ginger said to Adam, who confirmed the rumour with a nod of his head.

'Do I need to give a statement or anything?'

Again, the policemen laughed.

'No, son. Statements are only needed if the death is classed as suspicious. This one isn't. I'm afraid to say your pal had a bit too much to drink and sadly passed away by choking on his own vomit, according to the paramedics.'

'But, the state of the room…' Adam started.

'Aye, he was a messy boy, wasn't he?'

Adam stared at them, incredulous at what he was hearing.

'You're not even going to investigate it?'

'We just have. Haven't you been listening?'

'But…'

'Listen to us and listen well, young man. Believe it or not, we know what we're doing. Even though we owe you no explanation, here is one anyway. Last night, a bunch of young twenty-somethings were let off the leash at a swanky hotel with cheap booze. Your pal had too much and died as a result. Now, it's tragic, but, as you know, it's the Twelfth weekend and we have bigger fish to fry.'

Adam couldn't believe what he was hearing.

'Is that the reason why you two aren't doing your job properly?' he said, standing up. 'Are you annoyed that you're missing the marching bands and were sent to the countryside on a jolly?'

Sunglasses took a step closer.

'Now, listen here you, ye wee prick, that's enough. One more word and this will not end well for you.'

Ginger took a step forward too, as if to underline the point.

Colin smiled disarmingly at the policemen and led Adam up the steps.

'We've spoken to the lad at reception and we'll arrange for the body to be moved later today,' Ginger shouted after them. 'As you said, all our best men are busy with the nasty Orangemen today.'

The police officers strode to their car and gunned the engine, taking off down the driveway at pace, leaving nothing but a bad taste in Adam's mouth.

Adam threw himself onto the bed and fought back the tears. Tears of injustice. Tears for his friend who wasn't getting a fair hearing.

'There's no way Danny died from drinking too much,' Adam said, piquing Colin's attention.

'He could drink most of us under the table, that's for sure.'

'And, when I spoke to him not long before he stormed out, he seemed grand.'

Colin raised an eyebrow.

'Are you thinking there was foul play involved?'

Adam didn't know if he was being ridiculous. Surely no one here; his friends, anyone in this stately home, could be capable of *murder*, could they?

'It couldn't hurt to ask around, I guess,' Adam said. 'The police have made their minds up and we've got a day with nothing to do.'

'Are you saying what I think your saying?'

'That's right,' Adam nodded, standing up. 'Our Sherlock marathon is cancelled.'

8

WARDROBE CHOICES

EVERYONE GATHERED ON the spacious lawn at the front of the manor. Some sought the solace of shade that a smattering of ancient trees offered, their branches and foliage casting long shadows across the grass. Others basked in the mid-morning sun, content to confront the sun's rays head on in the hope of topping up a tan that would look good in the wedding photos.

If there even was a wedding.

Rumours had started to swirl at the first sighting of the police car. The sirens had barely stopped when ill-advised and ignorant whispers began.

Some concluded that Danny had been battered to death.

Some suggested that he'd died of a drug overdose – he had been known to dabble from time to time, after all.

Tragically, some of Danny's friends only found out about his untimely death by way of this gossip.

Sam and Emily – possible bride and groom-to-be – emerged from the entrance of the stately home, cutting Adam's thoughts on Danny short. Emily had arrived not long after the police had departed, and she and Sam had taken residence in the bridal suite, presumably discussing what to do next.

They weaved their way through the assembled groups on the lawn. Emily occasionally touched hands with one of her friends in way of hello while Sam stared straight ahead as he led his fiancée towards the decorative bandstand in the centre of the garden.

If this was on TV, Adam would've laughed at how overblown it seemed.

They walked up the steps and took their places in front of the crowd. Conversations hushed, and all eyes turned to the happy couple.

'Can everyone hear me?' Sam shouted, sounding like a headmaster at the front of an assembly hall.

Murmurs from all sides of the crowd suggested that yes, everyone could hear him.

'We're aware that people have been talking and we wanted to let you know exactly what has happened. I'm really sorry to say it, and it is heart-breaking, but Daniel Costello died in his sleep last night.'

Though most people already knew or had guessed, a gasp clouded Sam's next words. He paused to let everyone get it out of their systems.

'We've deliberated and, obviously what has happened is a terrible tragedy, but we've decided to press ahead with the wedding.'

Adam glanced around the crowd, wondering if this came as unwelcome news to anyone. All he saw was happiness.

He pulled on Colin's sleeve and signalled for his friend to follow him.

It was time to put a plan in place.

ADAM EMERGED FROM the bathroom with a flourish and a twirl.

Colin sat on the bed with a look of confusion etched on his face. He tried to focus on Adam but it was sensory overload.

His friend was wearing the clothes he'd been given for the wedding ceremony, given that he was part of the official wedding party - a navy three-piece suit combined with a plain white shirt and a red cravat. Pointed brown shoes completed his look.

'You're a day early,' Colin said.

'Wrong, old chap,' Adam replied. 'This is my detective outfit. Sherlock had a deerstalker and a pipe; I have a fashionable suit. You have to look official.'

'But what are you going to wear tomorrow? And, if we're actually going to do a bit of digging, we're going to be talking to our friends. Our friends who are all dressed super casually. You're going to get laughed at.'

Adam considered this.

'They won't if we are both wearing suits.'

Colin laughed.

'If you think I'm putting on a suit to go and talk to our friends, you've got another think coming. I'm dreading wearing one tomorrow, given the weather. I'm already sweating just thinking about it.'

'Fine,' Adam said, knowing that the matter was settled. 'Let's make a plan.'

WITH THE BEGINNINGS of a plan in place, Adam and Colin walked down the stairs and made their way up the lavish corridor towards Danny's room.

Step one, they had decided, was to take a good look at the body, just to confirm Adam's suspicions that foul play was indeed behind his passing. If Colin was unconvinced, they would abandon their folly and simply retire to their room to drown in episodes of Sherlock.

Colin made sure that no one was watching them while Adam pulled the handle, relieved to discover that the door had not been locked after the police's visit. Adam slinked into the room and Colin followed, easing the door closed with a gentle click.

Inside the room, the air was cloying and the heat held in by the heavy curtains that the police had redrawn before leaving felt oppressive. Adam wouldn't admit it, but he could feel the sweat gathering at his armpits under the woollen suit. He looks at his friend's casual get up – a T-shirt and shorts – with envy.

Colin flicked the light on and walked around the bed, getting his first glimpse of Danny's body. In his line of work, he had seen dead bodies before, but it never became any less shocking. This was different. This body belonged to someone he knew, someone who had their whole life ahead of him.

He scrunched up his nose to block out the smell of the vomit and tried to take in as many details from the body as he could.

'What do you think?' Adam asked.

'I agree with you, there's something fishy.'

Adam noticed details, as if for the first time. Details he must've taken in subconsciously when he discovered the body, enough to form initial suspicions.

A lump and a vivid purple bruise bloomed at the temple on the right side of Danny's face. A trickle of blood had escaped from a small cut in the same area, pooling on the pillow below his head.

Adam had to look away when he noticed this as he began to feel woozy. Colin pretended not to notice his friend recoil at the sight of the blood.

Another set of bruises, either side of the jaw, seemed to glow like beacons against the white of the face.

They look like finger marks, Colin thought. As if someone had grabbed him roughly.

Aside from that, and the tracks of vomit on his chin, there was nothing else to see.

Adam checked the windows, pleased to find that they were secured from the inside. That meant one thing. Whoever killed Danny came in through the door and left the same way. That meant that Danny had let them in.

'So, what do we do now?' Colin asked, taking one last look at the body and moving around the bed.

'We talk to the last person to see him alive. And thus, we begin our investigation.'

9

THE INVESTIGATION BEGINS

COLIN SAT ON a comfortable chair in the wide corridor outside his bedroom, looking out the huge bay window towards the sea.

Eternally pessimistic, he wondered how long it would be until the cliff receded far enough to drag the beautiful stately home towards the rocks and waves below it. A couple of hundred years, maybe?

He wondered if what they were about to do was worth the time and effort. Would their friends laugh in their faces as they played at being sleuths, trying to uncover something that wasn't there to be uncovered in the first place?

Surely, the police knew what they were talking about in matters of death. Though, the bruising on Danny's still face was troubling.

The door behind him creaked open and when he turned to the noise, he tried to hide his smirk as Adam emerged from their bedroom, dressed in shorts and a T-shirt, his suit discarded.

Adam gave his friend a look that told him he didn't want to hear any *I told you so's.*

'You were right,' he said simply. 'Now, time to start the case.'

'Do you know who the last person to see Danny alive was?' Colin asked, rising from his chair.

'I have my suspicions.'

Adam's mind drifted to hazy memories of the night before.

He'd watched from the bar as the argument in the shadows had played out, as Sam's push floored Danny. He'd watched Danny trudge out, stopping only to whisper in the ear of a girl on the dancefloor. Adam couldn't remember who.

Twenty minutes later, Sam had left the room. To Adam's eyes, it had seemed as if his best man had left a trail of breadcrumbs for him to follow. Sam hadn't deviated to the dancefloor though, instead marching straight through the heavy doors into the corridor outside.

'We start with Sam.'

'You don't think he could have killed Danny, do you?'

Adam looked his friend in the eye.

'Before this morning, I didn't think any of our friends could be capable of murder. But a dead body says otherwise.'

SAM WAS HOLED up in the bridal suite. When Adam knocked, Emily answered, a Cheshire cat smile plastered on her face, not managing to mask the worry behind it. Since their announcement at the bandstand, she'd changed into more casual attire.

'Sorry that things aren't going to plan,' Adam said. 'It must be a nightmare.'

'Something to tell the grand kids, eh?' she half laughed as she walked away from the door, back into the safety of the room. Adam didn't know if this was an invitation to follow her or not, but luckily Sam's appearance in the doorway meant he didn't make a fool of himself.

'Fancy a pint?' Adam asked.

Sam looked momentarily panicked, as if Adam had asked him to choose a drink with him over his wife-to-be. His alarm was short lived, as Emily reappeared and joked that taking Sam from under her feet would be brilliant, as she still had last minute bits and pieces to prepare for tomorrow.

He kissed her goodbye on the cheek and the three of them made their way down the stairs towards the bar, engaged in idle chit chat, skirting around the headline.

The barroom that the party had taken place in last night looked completely different in the cold light of day. The tables had been pushed back into place, covering over the sins committed on the dancefloor. The balloons and banners had all been taken down, returning the room to its original stately grace.

A grandfather clock in the corner of the room served as a reminder that it wasn't quite the afternoon yet.

Oblivious to its warning, Adam ordered three pints while Colin and Sam chose a table. He watched them converse freely with a feeling of unease spreading in his stomach – were they really going to question their friend in relation to murder?

With pints dished out, talk naturally turned to Danny. Generalities were explored first, before Adam's gentle attempts at probing earned a raised eyebrow from the groom.

'Look,' Adam stated, baldly. 'We think that, maybe, there's something more to Danny's death.'

'Something more, how?'

'Something suspicious.'

Sam looked sceptical.

Adam took up the mantle.

'The police said Danny died from drinking too much. For one, he didn't seem that drunk before he left here, and two, I've seen Danny drink enough to put me in a coma and still bag a girl at the end of a night out.'

'So, you're investigating?'

Adam's cheek reddened at the formality, and he saw Colin's eyes dip to the floor.

'We're... asking some questions.'

'You can't think I've got anything to do with it,' Sam scoffed. 'He was my best friend – my best man.'

'No, of course not,' said Colin, disarmingly. 'We just wanted to piece last night together - who had contact with him and things like that.'

Sam took a sip from his pint and nodded while Adam searched for the best opening question.

'Do you think anyone here would've wanted to harm Danny?'

'Yes. You know him, how abrasive he can be. He rubs people up the wrong way constantly and is always having scraps with anyone fool enough to rise to his crap. But, I can't see anyone killing him. He is...' Sam faltered. 'Was... annoying, but not to that extreme.'

'I saw you two have a bit of an argument over there,' said Adam, pointing to the corner of the room beyond the bar. 'What was that about?'

Sam looked as if he was vying for time, swilling the answer through his head before letting it escape his lips.

'He was just being a dick,' he said, finally. 'He'd had a few pints in him, and a couple of shots – we all had – and he was just being his usual annoying self. He was slabbering on about the wedding, about how Emily was stealing me and how he'd probably never see me again after the vows. It was pissing me off, so I told him to shut his mouth and gave him a shove. He left in a huff.'

'Did you see him again?'

'Yeah. When he didn't come back, I went looking for him to apologise. I went to his room and hammered at the door, but he wouldn't let me in.'

'So, you didn't see him again?'

'I'm getting to that,' he replied, testily. 'When he wouldn't let me in, I went down to reception and asked for a key to his room. I explained the situation, and the guy gave me it. I went back, unlocked the door and he was lying on the bed, texting someone. I apologised and so did he, and I left again.'

'Do you know who he was texting?'

Sam shook his head.

'Did he seem drunk to you?' Colin asked.

'No,' Sam said, still shaking his head. 'I mean, a bit. Not so drunk that he would've passed out.'

'What did you do after you left?'

'I went back to the party and stayed there until they stopped serving. I don't remember getting back to my room.'

'And the key?'

'I gave it to Ross. When Danny didn't come back to the party after our talk, I was going to go and see him again, to convince him to come back. Ross said not to bother, that he would go. I gave him the key and put the whole thing out of my mind.'

Sam finished his pint and looked at his watch.

'I best be getting back, I think. Emily will have a list of jobs the length of her arm for me. If you need anything else, give me a shout.'

'One last question,' Adam said, as Sam rose from his seat. 'Do you know anyone who would want the wedding called off?'

Sam looked aghast.

'No,' he said with a tone of finality. 'We've only invited people who mean something to us and who we care for. No one here would wish us harm. At least, I hope they wouldn't.'

They watched him walk away, his shoulders slightly slumped.

'It's time we visit the twin with the key,' Adam said, draining his glass.

9

A KICK IN THE BALEARICS

COLIN SANK ONTO the bed while Adam remained standing, pacing to and fro in front of the window, the glorious sunshine filtering in, turning him into a silhouette.

'What are you thinking?' Colin asked.

Adam stopped pacing. He mulled things over for a while, before sitting down on the end of the bed.

'Well, for one, I think the story he told us about why he and Danny argued was nonsense. He was always so tolerant of Danny, always sticking up for him and calming others down when his mouth got him into trouble. For Sam to lose it with him, whatever he was saying to him must've been really bad.'

'He looked put on the spot with that one too,' Colin added, thinking back to the pause he took before answering that particular question.

'I agree. The rest of the answers flowed straight off his tongue, but this one he had to think about. We need to find out what the real reason was for his reaction to Danny.'

'What about this key business?'

'It checks out, I reckon,' Adam said, 'though it would be good to check with whoever was at reception, to confirm.'

'Doesn't that go against confidentiality? I don't like the thought of someone snooping through my stuff.'

'He probably only did it because it was the groom. I can't imagine he'd go handing out keys willy-nilly. More than his job is worth.'

Before Colin could reply, his attention was snatched by movement outside. He got up from the bed and crossed to the window, sitting on the seat built into the bay. It offered him a perfect view of the lawn.

Crossing the recently cut grass was a girl. Her blonde hair appeared golden in the sunlight. She was wearing a pair of denim cut-off shorts and a bright, strappy vest top. From behind, it was difficult to make out who it was.

Plotting her path, it wasn't difficult to see where she was going. In the shade of the trees at the far end of the gardens was a swing seat, so far away the details of it were nigh on impossible to make out.

One thing *was* easy to see, though.

The lanky frame of the person sitting on it, watching the blonde advance towards him, was none other than Ross McMullan.

The next person they needed to speak to.

'I think you should lead the next one,' Adam said, following Colin's gaze.

'Why?'

'Well, we are a team. I led the first one and now it's your turn.'

'But, I don't...'

'Don't know what you're doing?' Adam finished. 'And I do? We're leading a murder investigation from things we've learned from the television. None of this is normal.'

'But you seem so confident.'

'Confidence is a shroud that allows the bearer to wear many faces.'

Colin looked impressed.

'Who said that?'

'I did, just then. Made it up. But it sounded impressive and that's all we can do – say things that sound good and hope that it tricks people into telling us what we want to know.'

Colin stood up and moved towards the door, ready.

'You sure you don't want to wear a suit for this?' Adam joked. His laugh was cut short when he saw Colin's narrowed eyes.

THEY WALKED ACROSS the garden, kicking clumps of cut grass to each other like footballers warming up before a match. Colin realised that he was feeling nervous and tried to think of the main points of questioning that he and Adam had gone over as they'd made their way downstairs from their room.

He wished he had a notebook to write things down in, but then, what they were doing was ridiculous enough already. The thought of pulling a notebook from his trouser pockets was a step too far.

Upon seeing them progress towards him, Ross struggled out of the fabric seat and extended a hand which both men shook. Ross stood awkwardly, stuck between retaking his place in the swing seat and seeming childish, or standing like an adult should when a discussion was clearly on the horizon.

In the end, he stood.

He reached into the back pocket of his chino shorts and pulled out a packet of cigarettes, taking one out and flicking the box towards Adam and Ross like an invitation. Both declined.

'I forgot you both gave up,' mumbled Ross, through lips clamped tight against the stick of nicotine. 'I don't know how you do it.'

Colin was appreciative of the slight gusts of wind that were playing with Ross's lighter, causing it to flicker and extinguish just before fulfilling its purpose. It allowed him time to get his head right and size up his opponent.

'Must be a bit weird, seeing your brother marry a girl you went out with once,' Colin said, pleased with his opening gambit.

'Not really. It was so long ago and we only went on a few dates,' Sam countered, turning his attention back to his cigarette struggles.

'It's mad about Danny, isn't it?' Colin pressed on.

'Crazy. I can't believe it. Rumours are floating round that you two don't buy what the police have said. I hear you've questioned the groom. Is that why you're here talking to me? Am I under arrest?'

Before Colin or Adam could answer, Ross laughed at his own joke.

'Ask away. I think it's a silly way to spend a Saturday and a complete waste of time, but we all like different things.'

'We'd like to hear about the argument that you stopped last night between Danny and Sam. We've heard Sam's version of it, but we'd like to hear yours too.'

Ross arched an eyebrow.

'Sam told you?'

'Yeah,' Colin said, surprised at how easily the lie slipped off his tongue.

'Flip,' Ross said. 'I thought he was trying to keep that as secret as possible, but I guess you're his friends. He can trust you.'

He took one last puff on his cigarette before stubbing it out in the bucket of sand at the side of the swing. He sat down on the grass and motioned for Adam and Colin to follow suit. He cast a conspiratorial glance around the trees, as if they could be enemies eavesdropping in plain sight.

'It's true. Danny saw him cheat on Emily on his stag do. He'd been lording it over him since, threatening to tell people if Sam didn't buy him a pint or drive him wherever he needed to go. Stupid little things, really.'

He sighed deeply and took the packet of cigarettes out again, before reconsidering and throwing them onto the grass beside him instead, before continuing his story.

'I was supposed to be best man, but it got changed to Danny shortly after we all came back from Ibiza. Sam told me the reason; about the girl and how Danny was blackmailing him into making him best man. He apologised and begged me not to make a big deal about it otherwise people would start asking questions and the truth would come out.'

'And that's what the argument was about?' Colin asked.

'Yeah,' he said. 'Danny was mouthing off again, and it was the straw that broke the camel's back. Sam snapped and shoved him. Danny gave him a look as he was leaving that worried Sam, so he went after him not long after in a panic. He was worried that Danny was going to blab to anyone who would listen.'

'Do you know what happened when he went to see him?'

'He came back looking much calmer. He said he'd sorted it and that he'd go back later to check again. He put up a bit of fuss when I told him to enjoy his night and that I'd check in later instead.'

'And did you?'

He looked sheepish.

'I was going to. Sam gave me the spare key to his room. I put it in my jacket pocket and then we all went on the dancefloor – the Macarena, ya know? Hard to resist.'

They all nodded in agreement. The song seemed to possess some sort of gravitational pull towards the nearest dancefloor.

'Anyway, when we were finished, I put my jacket on and went to Danny's room. When I checked my pocket, the key wasn't there.'

'Someone had taken it?'

He nodded.

'And it's still missing?'

Another nod.

'Did Danny let you in?'

'No,' he said. 'I banged on the door, but he never answered. I could hear the TV was on, so I assumed he was in there, but I've just chatted to Vicky and apparently he paid her a visit last night.'

'Vicky?' Colin and Adam said in unison.

Of course, the blonde they had observed walking across the grass earlier. Danny's ex-girlfriend.

'It might be worth having a chat with her,' Ross said. 'Big news there.'

10

EX'S AND OH'S

HAVING DISCUSSED THE upcoming football season and listened to Ross's pessimistic views on Preston's promotion chances, they left him to it. When they looked back, he'd settled back into his swing seat with a fresh cigarette, sunglasses on and head tilted back. Presumably, once they were out of sight, he'd be texting around, warning people that a couple of amateur sleuths were in town.

'Did you believe him?' Colin asked.

Adam nodded.

'I think the fact that he told us the real reason behind the fight shows that we can trust him, even if it was taken by questionable means...'

Colin glanced over at him, pleased to see that his impressed expression negated his words.

'Very tricksy,' Adam said. 'Sadly, the chat raised more questions than answers.'

'How so?'

'Firstly, why did Sam lie about the reason behind the fight? Does he have something to hide? Secondly, Ross looked pretty miffed that he missed out on being his brother's best man. Might he have had something to do with bumping off his competitor who took the title by means of blackmail? Finally, who has the room key? Whoever has that surely is the person behind the murder.'

Colin looked jaded at how little they'd achieved so far. It felt like gardening – however many weeds you ripped from the ground, there were always more waiting to spring from the gaps you'd created.

'The method of murder also remains a mystery,' Adam added, piling more onto Colin's already full plate. 'He wasn't battered to death, which means that it wasn't a crime of passion – the police would've spotted any outward damage. Which means that whoever killed him had planned it, which very much rules Sam and Ross in.'

'Both had means,' Colin agreed. 'One was being blackmailed on threat of a secret being exposed and the other was seeing his twin suffer, having had his best man title taken from him.'

Frustration rose in the air between them.

'The only way is forward,' Adam said. 'Let's go see what Vicky's breaking news is.'

VICKY WATSON WAS surprised to see the two men outside her door, but stood aside to let them in anyway, at Adam's request. Having always had a slight crush on her, Colin kept his gaze low, focusing instead on the rough grain of the floorboards.

The door clicked behind her and she made her way to the corner of the room, throwing herself into a velvet chair next to a writing desk. From it, she took a bottle of water and guzzled thirstily from it.

Colin snuck a glance in her direction, pity panging in his chest. Judging from the mascara smudged below her bloodshot eyes, whatever news she had to impart was not good.

Adam took in the room. It was almost identical to theirs; similar abstract art on the walls and a large window with a view that matched theirs. The big difference was that her room had two single beds.

A light bulb illuminated in Adam's mind. But first, to business.

'Vicky, we've come to speak to you about Danny.'

She sniffed, trying to hold back a sob, but to no avail. The floodgates burst open and she let out a wail.

Both men's eyes widened in alarm as they looked at each other, both pleading silently with the other to be the one to do something about it. Eventually, Colin rolled his eyes and got up from the bed, tiptoeing towards her slowly as one might approach a wild animal that might lash out at any second.

He tore a tissue for a box that was sitting on the table and reached it to her. She accepted with a quiet thank you before blowing her nose and placing the used tissue in the bin at her feet. She took a minute to compose herself, apologised and fixed them with a sad smile.

'What do you want to talk about Danny for?' she asked.

'Well, obviously you heard about what happened to him…'

She confirmed that she had with a slight nod of her head.

'…Well, we don't think that it was accidental. We think someone meant to kill him, so we're asking around. Someone hinted that you might have some information.'

'Ross,' she said. A statement, rather than a question.

'Can you tell us what you know?'

'As you know, Danny and I went out for about a while, about three years ago. He broke up with me and we started seeing new people. My mum and dad hated him, so it was never going to last, and I was quite relieved when he ended it. About three weeks ago, he started texting me again, completely out of the blue. Maybe he thought that there was a chance of seeing each other at the wedding and he was getting his feelers out early.'

'Did you text back?'

'Yes, but only a few times. I told him I had a boyfriend and that it was inappropriate for him to be contacting me. It didn't stop him. In fact, not even my boyfriend ringing him put him off, even though Neil gave him a right old shouting at.'

'Where is Neil?'

'He was here last night, but had to leave after the party because he was working today. He's coming back tonight… I hope.'

With that, she burst into tears again. This time, they let her get it out of her system without interfering. She wiped at her eyes, smearing black across her cheeks like warpaint.

'Why wouldn't he come back?' Adam asked when he thought it was safe.

'Because… I slept with Danny once he'd left. He'd said sorry downstairs at the party for texting, and told me to pass his apologies onto Neil. He'd already gone by this point. At the end of the night, there was a knock on my door. It was Danny. I was drunk and I didn't know what I was doing, but I let him in. He seemed… pleased with himself.'

'What do you mean?'

'You know, the usual Danny Costello swagger – boasting about this and that, and he was walking with a spring in his step.'

This news was unexpected. According to Sam, Danny was pissed off and cooped up in his room, still feeling stung about their argument. Although, him being up here, propositioning his ex-girlfriend explained where he was when Ross went a-knocking.

'Did he say why?'

'We didn't say much at all, if you get my drift…'

Something permeated the room – an awkwardness that Adam felt he could almost decant from the air and bottle. It hung thick around them.

'Do you remember what time this was?'

Colin asked the question, his words acting as a welcome candle in the dark.

'He came up at just after one o'clock and left at about quarter past. He didn't hang around.'

'And that's why you're worried Neil might not come?' Colin said.

She nodded, fresh tears forming in the corners of her eyes.

'Is there anything else that happened?'

'Actually, yeah,' she said, straightening up in her chair. 'When he was putting on his jacket, after… you know… an envelope fell out. It was open at the top, but I couldn't see what was in it. Though, when it dropped on the floor, it sounded heavy.'

'Heavy?'

'Yeah, it was loud. It didn't bang, it sounded more like a slap. Like it was full of folded paper or something.'

A physical clue – interesting.

With nothing more to go on, they left Vicky's room and were half way down the corridor when Adam turned back, hammering on the door again. Vicky opened it, tears flowing like a river down her cheeks.

'I was just wondering if... well...'

He paused, wondering how to word it to keep the offence to a minimum.

'Spit it out,' she said.

'Well, our room has one double bed and you have two singles. I'm assuming that, after what happened last night, Neil won't be coming tonight, so was wondering if you fancied swapping rooms? It'd make our lives so much easier.'

The door slammed shut in Adam's face milliseconds after he finished asking the question. Colin dragged him away before Vicky returned with something sharp.

'Idiot,' his friend said, punching him on the arm.

11

ANOTHER SNOOP

'WELL, ONE THING is for certain,' Adam said, while unlocking the bedroom. 'If Danny was sober enough to, you know...'

He made a crude hand gesture which caused Colin shake his head.

'...for a bit of how's your mother,' he continued, noting his friend's displeasure. 'It meant he definitely couldn't have been drunk enough to choke on his vomit.'

It was an interesting idea, Colin thought as he followed Adam into the room. He threw himself onto the bed; the traipsing around the long corridors mingling with the stupefying heat caused a sudden wave of exhaustion.

'Do we have time for a rest?' Colin asked, stifling a yawn.

Adam checked the time and shook his head.

'I've got a theory. I think someone did this to stop the wedding.'

Colin was unconvinced, but waved his hand at Adam for elaboration.

'If whoever killed Danny did it for that reason, it didn't work. The wedding is happening tomorrow, which means whoever did the killing may do more. We're working under a time constraint here.'

He sat down on the bed too and threw his eyes towards the ceiling.

'What I've realised is just how amateur we've been so far,' he said. 'We looked a bit at Danny's face, which didn't help us work out how he'd been killed. I think what we need to do is search his room. We know he had an envelope, but we don't know what was in it. Perhaps, whoever killed him was after whatever was inside.'

He thought for a few more minutes.

'We're going to split up. You go and search the room while I do a bit of work elsewhere.'

'Why do I have to search the room?' Colin asked, the colour rising in his cheeks. The thought of spending another second in the room with Danny's corpse caused a shiver to run through his spine.

'Well, you're used to bodies, in your line of work and…'

'You're a wimp,' interrupted Colin.

Adam was in no position to argue. Colin accepted his mission with a small nod of the head.

'What am I looking for?' he asked, rising from the bed.

'The envelope and anything that seems out of the ordinary,' Adam said, unhelpfully. 'Check anywhere you think something might be hidden. Desk drawers or in the suitcase, that kind of thing.'

Colin left the room with a sense of unease. How were they supposed to solve a crime, if they didn't even know what they were looking for?

He trudged down the corridor, hoping that some sort of Spidey-sense would awaken within him, though he didn't hold out much hope. He made his way down the grand staircase and passed a few people sitting in groups around tables in the foyer, catching snippets of conversation, all about the stricken best man.

He made his way down the corridor towards Danny's room, turning back every few steps to make sure no one was following him. The last thing he needed was company, or even worse, someone mistaking his meddling as guilt. Visiting the room once was a risk, let alone venturing in again with no suitable explanation as to why if he were to be questioned.

Casting one last clandestine look around, he slipped in the door, a sense of déjà vu enveloping him. Everything was as they'd left it.

The lifeless body was still on the bed; the bruises unmoved, though slightly darker, and the vomit uncleaned. Perhaps the police had instructed the hotel staff to leave the room untouched until after the body was collected.

Colin scanned around. He ignored the light switch for fear of alerting someone to the room, instead letting his eyes adjust to the dusky hues. He made his way to the middle and turned a full circle, hoping for some little detail to leap out at him.

Nothing did.

Instead, he moved over to the body and rooted through the pockets of his jacket and trousers. Inside, there were a few card receipts from the bar last night, but nothing of great importance.

Something else caught his attention.

The smell.

At first, as on the previous times, the overriding smell was that left behind from the vomit. But underneath it was something else, something smoky, medicinal almost.

Whiskey.

A small grain of doubt fell into the cogs of Colin's thinking, causing them to shudder to a stop.

The whiskey, coupled with the vomit, was a very obvious sign that pointed to an accidental death. If it weren't for Adam's persistence that something was amiss in all of this, Colin would've downed tools there and then.

Instead, he pressed on.

For a while, he searched in drawers, pushing the contents this way and that, coming away empty each time. He moved from desk to bedside cabinet to wardrobe, but there was no sign of anything suspicious.

Frustration rose like a beast inside him.

Why had Adam sent him on a fool's errand?

The silence in the room was interrupted by voices in the hallway outside. Voices that were growing louder by the second. Panicking, Colin crossed the bedroom in three giant strides, rushing into the bathroom and closing the door as quietly as he could behind him.

He stepped into the bath and pulled the shower curtain, wincing as the metallic rings scraped against the curtail rail. Visions of Psycho plagued him as he waited with his breath held.

Outside the bathroom door, two men were talking. From what he could make out, they were here to collect the body. They quickly discussed how they were going to move it, before putting the plan into action. Colin heard grunting, the rustle of fabric and a quiet bang as something fell over.

'You've knocked the bin over,' said one of the voices.

'Ah, the cleaners will get it later,' replied the other.

The voices were muffled as the sound of the bedroom door slamming filled the room. After that, Colin heard no more, though he didn't move from his spot for a few minutes, just in case. When he was sure the coast was clear, he scurried out of the bath and splashed water over his sweating face at the sink.

He grabbed a handful of paper towels and dabbed them on his brow before looking around, dismayed to find nowhere to put the sopping material. He walked into the bedroom and saw the upturned bin, stopping short when he registered the contents strewn across the floor.

Next to the desk was a tattered brown envelope and the empty silver packaging of painkillers.

He lifted the envelope first, smoothing the creases and returning it to as near its original state as possible. There was nothing on the outside to mark it as different to the millions of other massed produced envelopes currently in circulation.

He turned it in his fingers before reaching inside. Whatever was in there to make it heavy was now gone. In its place was a single piece of paper, its thin blue lines scrawled over in black biro. The hand that wrote it appeared both rushed and angry to Colin's mind.

He took in the message, turning it around in his head in order to try to make some sense of it, before shoving the missive back inside the envelope and the envelope inside the pocket of his shorts.

Next, he lifted the silver packaging. It belonged to regular paracetamol, though all eight blisters were empty. There was also no sign of the box from which they'd been procured.

Which made sense.

Danny would have no reason to own a box of paracetamol, since he was allergic to them.

Colin rose from the floor, eager to get back to Adam to discuss the things he'd found. As he moved towards the door, a quiet beep emitted from somewhere nearby.

Colin tried to zone in on where it had come from.

Getting down on his knees, he groped around under the bed, his hand settling on only cobwebs and lumps of dust. He moved around to the other side of the bed and repeated the task.

This time, his fingers touched something small and rectangular. He pulled it out from under the bed and held it in the shaft of light coming through the curtains.

It was a phone.

But not the up-to-date iPhone Danny made sure to get on release day.

It was a thin Nokia, as nondescript as they come. A small black-and-white screen told him that the battery was low. He dismissed the message with the click of a button, pocketed it and left the room, aware more than ever that time may be slipping away from them.

12

TUBTHUMPING

ONCE COLIN HAD left, Adam had a quick lie down. He felt bad, leaving his friend to do the legwork in the room, but he really couldn't face seeing the body again.

He also felt bad, knowing that he'd sent his friend on what could be a wild goose chase. There might be nothing incriminating in the room, but if there was, he fully trusted his friend to find it.

As partners went, he'd pick Colin every day of the week. He was loyal, trusting, and had stuck up for Adam since their first day at primary school together. He had a big heart, as evidenced by the job he'd chosen – a job not many other twenty-something year old lads would be seen dead doing. He was clever too – cleverer than he thought he was. He just needed some confidence.

Pushing Colin out of his mind and letting Danny in, he considered what came next. The case (he still felt weird calling it that) was progressing nicely, though it was becoming hard to keep track of the comings and goings. He resolved to fix that.

Jumping up from the bed, he grabbed the key from the sideboard and marched towards the door.

ADAM LOOKED AROUND the library. It was a nice space, not anything grand like the rest of the house, but rather cosy. All four walls were lined with bookcases that stretched from floor to ceiling, an elaborate chandelier casting sprinkles of light across the dark wood.

A wide selection of books filled the shelves; the cracked spines hinting that they had been well thumbed by many a visitor. It was a nice touch, having this room readily available in a place so remote. The solitude of the house probably seemed perfect for a getaway, but after a few days, Adam could imagine the books acted as a welcome distraction.

He moved the mouse in order to bring the computer screen to life. He tapped a few buttons, logging in with the details he'd been given at reception, before navigating to Facebook. He was a reluctant social media user, but the website was all he needed right now.

For ten minutes, he searched for what he required and collected his printing from the machine in the corner of the room.

Pulling the door open, he left the room, colliding with a solid mass that caused him to fall to the floor, his papers dropping around him like snow.

'Sorry, man,' said Mike, offering a hand and pulling Adam to standing. 'Didn't see you there.'

Adam took him in as he bent down and began collecting the papers. Mike, the bride's brother, had been in the same year as Adam, but was never in his friendship group. He'd been a sort of loner, regularly eating his lunch in the toilets, making him easy fodder for the bullies who'd made his school life miserable. He'd used university as a chance for change, emerging with muscles Arnie would be proud and a new found sense of confidence, as evidenced by the clothes he chose to wear.

Mike handed Adam the pieces of paper he'd scooped up without comment.

'How are you feeling today?' Adam asked, folding the wad of paper and putting it in his pocket.

'Alright,' Mike said, curiosity clouding his features.

'You were pretty smashed last night,' Adam elaborated.

'Oh, that. Yeah,' Mike laughed. 'I had a blast, from what I can remember, anyway.'

'I didn't think Emily's side of the family were coming until tonight.'

'We had a family meal at the house, and then Emily and her bridesmaids went off to sort what colour their nails were going to be. It was either sit around on my own or come to the party.'

'Party wins every time,' Adam said.

'Indeed it does,' chuckled Mike, before turning serious. 'Pretty bad about Danny. I felt awful for Emily when I heard – she's been planning this day since she was a wee girl. I heard you are doing a bit of detective work.'

Adam confirmed he was with an embarrassed half nod.

'Good man, yourself,' he said. 'If you find out who did it, give him an extra slap from me. The last thing my family needed was more stress on the eve of the wedding.'

Adam was about to tell him that he hoped it would never come to blows, but Mike was already saying that he'd see him at the dinner tonight while wandering off towards the stairs.

ADAM RETURNED TO the room to find Colin slumped in the seat, swigging from the hipflask he'd been given by Sam. The red blotches on his cheeks against the pallor of his skin suggested he had a story to tell, which he dutifully launched into.

'Jesus,' exclaimed Adam, his eyes wide at the thought of Colin nearly being caught snooping around.

Just you wait, thought Colin. He hadn't even got around to telling his friend what he'd uncovered.

From his pocket, he took the envelope. He set it on the table, letting Adam examine it. He imagined this is how going on the Antiques Roadshow felt.

Adam picked the envelope up, casting his gaze over the outside. There was no name, address or stamp, which meant that the envelope must've been delivered by hand.

Next, he examined the opening at the top. To Adam's eye, it seemed to have been ripped in haste. The line was not cleanly torn, as it would've been if a letter opener had been used.

No, this was done with speed.

Out of fear?

Perhaps

Or excitement, as dirty deeds often are.

Fishing inside, his fingers settled on nothing but the scrap of paper. The same scrap of paper that had made Colin's heart gallop not twenty minutes previously.

Unfolding the paper, he read the scribbled words.

£200. And that's the last of it, as agreed.

'The last of it?' Adam said. 'That would suggest that whoever gave this to Danny has given him more in the past.'

'And that would suggest that whoever gave him the money also had cause to kill him,' Colin added. 'But, why would anyone be giving him money?'

'To shut him up,' Adam said. 'We know he blackmailed Sam into giving him the best man gig. What if he was blackmailing someone else too?'

'Or, what if he wasn't?'

'You think Sam did this?'

Colin shrugged.

'It makes sense. Danny has been threatening to expose Sam's secret kiss. What happened if Sam snapped and decided enough was enough after the argument?'

Adam considered it. It made sense, but the timeframe seemed too quick for Sam to have committed the murder. They knew that Danny paid Vicky a visit after he'd seen Sam, so he was definitely alive when the groom had left. Could Sam have snuck back later in the night? Had he been the one who had stolen the key from Ross's jacket? It certainly was a possibility – after all, no one else knew about the spare key.

When Adam made no reply, Colin took out the second thing he'd found.

The empty strip of tablets.

'Why would these be in his room? He's allergic,' Adam said, twirling the packet in his fingers, the light reflecting off the silver packaging.

'You think that's how he was killed? Someone made him take the tablets that they knew he'd have a reaction to?' Colin asked.

Adam gave no answer, keen not to jump to conclusions, though the reasoning seemed watertight.

Danny had been allergic to paracetamol his whole life. After many a night out, he'd lamented his allergy as a curse; the hangover inevitable, to be endured without treatment. It was a well-known ailment and something that could be easily used against him.

It didn't help narrow down the culprit.

Adam moved it to the side, leaving a space for the final piece of evidence. Colin dutifully set the antiquated phone between them.

Adam looked at it with curiosity, his eyes narrowing.

'A burner?' he said.

The prominence and use of burner phones – disposable devices that aided with anonymity when committing nefarious deeds – were a mainstay of nearly every Hollywood film that had a crime in it.

'That's what I guessed,' Colin nodded.

Adam picked it up, pleased to find that it didn't have a passcode. Danny probably thought that he and it would never be apart, and so saw no need for added security.

Adam navigated through the menus to the call list, unsurprised to find it empty. Next, he moved to the messages. The sent box was empty but there was a two-word message in the inbox, received at 12:51 a.m.

I'm here.

Adam held the screen towards Colin, watching his friend's eyes as he tried to make sense of the message.

'So, he arranged to meet someone? I assume that's when the money was handed over.'

Adam nodded.

'That would make sense. He took the envelope, checked the money was all there, then went straight to Vicky to flaunt his wad.'

'Adam!' scolded Colin.

'I'm talking about the money!' replied Adam.

'So, who sent the message?' Colin asked, getting back on track.

'That, Watson, is what we need to find out next.'

Colin closed his eyes and tried to plot out their next move. He also wondered why he was Watson and not Sherlock.

Adam spoke, tearing him from his thoughts.

'I've got something to do here,' he said, pointing to the pile of printed papers. 'Can you go and speak to whoever is on reception?'

Colin nodded, realising exactly why he was Watson while Adam continued.

'Find out if the person who was on the desk last night at 12:51 a.m. is about. Ask them if they saw Danny.'

'Surely he would've done his deal in secret, in some hidden corner,' Colin interjected.

Adam nodded.

'I would agree if I thought whoever sent that text was already in the building.'

'You think someone travelled here to give Danny the money?'

Adam nodded again.

'I do. I think if it was someone who was already here, they wouldn't have bothered with phones and messages. Too much of a data trail. I think he had to have the phone to get in touch with whoever came here to hand him that envelope. I think, after seeing the phone, that we can conclude that he was blackmailing more than just Sam. We just need to find out who.'

13

A SIGHTING AND A MONSTROUS USE OF BLU TACK

COLIN LEFT THE bedroom and wandered down the expansive corridor once more. He felt like he'd walked the hallways so many times that, should they need a tour guide in the near future, he would be in pole position for that job.

Once more, he descended the staircase with burning hamstrings, eyeing who was on the front desk as he did so.

It was a dark-haired man. Not the same one who had greeted them with a single key on arrival. This man was a little shorter with a clean-shaven face. Colin watched him converse with one of Emily's friends, his movements fluid as he took a key out of a drawer and passed it to her at the same time as telling her the directions to her room.

Colin waited until she'd gathered up her suitcases.

Plural.

A lot of luggage for two night's stay, he thought to himself as she walked away, wheeling one case while hoisting a smaller bag onto her shoulder.

'How can I help you?' the man behind the desk said. His accent suggested he originally came from Belfast way.

Colin stepped forward.

'I'm wondering if you know who was working on the desk last night?' he said.

'That was me,' the man said, extending his hand across the desk. 'James Miller.'

Colin shook his hand.

'I was wondering if you saw my friend…'

James's gaze diverted from him and Colin realised that someone had joined the queue behind him. James smiled at Colin.

'I think I know what you want to talk about.' He checked his watch. 'I'm about to clock off. Why don't you meet me outside and I can answer some of your questions?'

Colin nodded and stood aside, letting an older lady pass by him. He turned and walked through the huge door, coming to rest on the steps outside. He squinted into the sunlight, wishing he'd had the foresight to bring his sunglasses with him.

WHILE COLIN WAS watching the few clouds in the sky drift lazily past, Adam was busy in the room. He moved from table to wall, picking up a piece of paper, pressing some Blu Tack onto the back of it before sticking it onto the wall. Police officers usually had a case board, one that they could wheel about easily and add to when needed, but this would do for now.

When he had exhausted his pile of paper, he stood back and took his creation in. It may not be pretty, but it was already helping him to piece together the case like a jigsaw. He just needed to voice his theory aloud.

For that, he needed his partner.

COLIN JUMPED AS James tapped his shoulder. He had been thinking about everything and nothing, lost in the haze and heat of the day. Thoughts worked their way back and forth through his head; stupidity and embarrassment that he'd agreed to undertake the task of detective at all. Every time he had to ask questions, he felt like a boy playing a game with grown-ups who were simply humouring him. On the other hand, he'd managed to uncover definite clues that suggested that Danny was murdered.

James sat down beside him on the step, pulling a cigarette out. He offered one to Colin, who declined, before lighting his own.

'So, it was you who was working last night?' Colin asked.

James nodded, exhaling a plume of acrid smoke.

'We're always short staffed around this time of year, on account of the parades, which I have no interest in,' he explained. 'It means working a late night and an early morning, but I'm alright with that for the overtime pay.'

'And you thought you might've seen my friend who died?'

'Sorry to hear he was your mate,' James said, nodding. 'I'm sure it was him, because I was the one who showed the police to his room this morning. I recognised him immediately.'

'Why?' Colin asked. Danny didn't really have any distinguishing features to speak off; nothing that made him stand out from the crowd.

'Because I remember thinking last night that he seemed like he was up to something. He was loitering in the reception and when I asked him if he needed anything, he shook his head. He seemed like this bag of directionless energy. Then, his phone rang and he ran outside.'

'And you didn't see what he was up to outside.'

'No,' he answered, shaking his head. 'Like I said, we're short staffed and I'm not meant to leave the desk. I assumed he had gone to meet a girl or something. I didn't think any more of it until he came in again a few minutes later.'

He stopped to take another puff of his cigarette, which was burning close to his fingers. Colin remained silent, afraid he'd interrupt the thread of the story.

'When he came back in, he seemed changed. The frenzy of before was gone, replaced with... swagger, maybe,' he said, shrugging his shoulders.

'What do you mean?'

'I mean, he came in with his shoulders rolling, like he thought he was the big man. He was holding an envelope and going through whatever was inside. I was about to ask, because I was worried it was drugs, but he was gone before I could say anything.'

'Did anything else happen with him?'

'No,' he said, throwing his cigarette on the step and stamping on it, before lifting it again. 'I shouldn't leave that there. More than my job's worth!'

Colin thanked him and stood to leave.

'Oh, one more thing, actually,' James said. 'After he put the envelope away, he walked upstairs. I heard him talking to someone, another lad, sounded like a bit of an argument. I couldn't hear what they were saying, only the tone of the conversation and it wasn't friendly.'

He stood and began walking towards a red Corsa.

'Now, if you'll excuse me, it's time I got some shut eye.'

COLIN'S FACE FELL when he took in what Adam had been up to in his absence.

The wall was covered in paper, pages and pages of it. Pictures of people and a bird's-eye view of the manor house were connected with pieces of red string.

'Please tell me you haven't used Blu Tack to stick that up?' Colin said.

'Why?'

'It stains the wall. I don't fancy paying some bill to have it cleaned.'

Adam waved his concerns away with a flick of his wrist. He stood slightly to the side of his masterpiece, and Colin saw the glint in his eye that preceded a show. He pulled the chair out from below the table and sat down in front of the mass of paper, feeling very much like a pupil in Adam's classroom.

Before Adam began, he asked his friend to give him the skinny on what he'd found out from the receptionist. As he relayed his story, Colin thought that the information he was giving was slotting nicely into whatever theory Adam had conjured up in his absence, judging from the look on his face.

'No CCTV?' Adam asked when Colin had finished.

His friend's face fell.

'I didn't check.'

'Luckily, I did. Yesterday. There aren't any cameras on the exterior and none that I can see in the inside either. Do you want to hear what I've come up with?'

Colin nodded.

'Now,' said Adam, assuming a theatrical air. 'I'm not saying this is what happened or anything, only what I've managed to piece together.'

He pointed first to the pictures of the people he'd stuck up – profile pictures from Facebook, judging by the varied poses and locations of the photos.

Colin took in the list of suspects.

Sam, the blackmailed groom.

Ross, the twin who lost out on being best man.

Vicky, the ex-girlfriend who Danny had sex with.

Neil, Vicky's boyfriend who may or may not have known about his girlfriend's infidelity.

'I printed these off before finding out about the phone, so my theory has changed slightly. I still think it could be any one of these, but I think they are working with someone.'

'Who?'

'Whoever came by car and gave Danny the cash. There's no way of telling who that is yet.'

Colin mulled it over. It would make sense that whoever handed the money over would be behind the murder. But he knew it couldn't physically be that person because the receptionist heard them drive away. Could they have teamed up with someone in the house to get their money back and take away any further blackmailing opportunities?

'Makes sense,' Colin said, eyes focussed on the wall again. 'Is there anyone we can rule out?'

Adam considered this.

'I think we should keep them all in mind at the minute, but Neil is probably the easiest to rule out. The rest were definitely in the house and aware of Danny wronging them in some way. Neil was probably on his way home, oblivious to his girlfriend cheating on him. If only we had CCTV, we could clarify a few things.'

'I know where we can go,' Colin said, his eyes widening. 'But first, get the Blu Tack off the walls.'

14

LIFE THROUGH A LENS

'WE COULD'VE WALKED,' Colin said, watching the blur of hedgerows and sheep out of the passenger side window. 'It's really not that far.'

Keeping his eyes on the narrow road, Adam tapped the digital clock in the middle of the dashboard.

'Time is of the essence, dear boy,' he said. 'If someone intends to cancel the wedding through another act of violence, I think they will do it tonight. That means we must act swiftly.'

It sounded impressive, but unconvincing. Adam could feel the withering look his friend was giving him.

'And it's hot and I'm lazy, alright. Give me a break.'

Instead of turning left out of the stately home's long driveway, they'd turned right. Colin had protested that the petrol station was the other way, but Adam had held up an annoying, placating hand without parting with further explanation.

For a few miles they travelled at a steady pace, passing nothing but farms and fields of animals. A dog had chased the car half-heartedly for less than twenty seconds, running out of steam at the bottom of a small incline.

Eventually, Adam indicated into a driveway and turned the car, travelling back in the direction they'd just come from.

'I just wanted to make sure that there were no main roads nearby that could've been used to access our hotel. When we look at the CCTV, if he lets us see it, we can be sure that coming past the petrol station was the only way to get to the hotel – and to Danny.'

They made their way down the road, past the hotel, and pulled into the empty forecourt of the petrol station, coming to a stop at one of the two pumps.

Adam got out, twisted the petrol cap and inserted the pump. He put some diesel in, mindful of his limited funds, and replaced the pump before walking across the oil-stained concrete and into the building.

A woman with grey, frizzy hair sat behind the counter, separated from the customers by a wall of glass. Her brown eyes were magnified by oversized glasses, lending her a rather comical appearance.

Adam walked up to her with a disarming smile plastered on his face. He slipped a note into the cut-out section and watched her check that it was real by gliding a pen across its surface. Happy, she rang the register and set the note in.

'Anything else, dear?' she asked with a smile.

He leaned conspiratorially towards her.

'I don't suppose you heard about what happened up at Milton Manor last night?'

Sorrow pulled her features into a sympathetic frown.

'Yes, dear,' she nodded gravely. 'There have been a few youngsters down from there today to buy cigarettes and cheaper alcohol than they serve up at that place. I heard a young boy died.'

Adam confirmed the story with a nod, trying to figure out how to get around to his request. It was Colin who broke the silence.

'Daniel was a good friend of ours. He was due to be best man at the wedding. The police think that his death was accidental, but we believe it might've been something more sinister than that.'

'Oh, God,' she gasped. 'How do you mean?'

Adam held back a smile. Colin knew that old people loved a bit of gossip. What he'd just done was plonk a metaphorical pile of gold on her counter, just out of reach. All they needed to do now was let her know that they'd nudge it her way if she gave them something in exchange.

'That's what we're trying to find out,' Colin continued. 'You see, we're following a few leads...'

'I thought you said the police had drawn their conclusion already,' she interrupted.

'We're not the police, we're…'

'…private investigators,' Adam finished. 'And we'd like to look at your CCTV cameras, if we could. We believe it could help us crack the case.'

SHE STUDIED THE lads through the glass. She'd watched a lot of detective dramas over the years and these two young fellas, in their shorts and T-shirts, didn't look much like real detectives. They usually wore suits. But then, nothing this exciting ever happened around these parts and they seemed like nice boys. If she could play a small part in solving a case, she'd do it.

She looked out of the window to make sure no one was on the forecourt before summoning them around the counter and into the back room.

THE ROOM WAS not very big and what little space there was, was taken up by excess stock. On a small desk, next to a door on the back wall, was a monitor. Black-and-white footage played on it in real time, judging by the date and time stamp in the bottom left-hand corner of the screen. A computer hummed steadily under the desk, the blue light around the power button casting some brightness into the otherwise gloomy room.

'My son set this up after someone filled their tank and did a runner. I have no idea how to use it, but I'm sure you will. Your generation are much better at these things than us old fogies.'

She left and reappeared a few minutes later, carrying two bottles of water.

'For the workers,' she said with a smile as she set the bottles on the table. She checked if they wanted anything else and when they declined, she left them to it.

Adam hunkered down in front of the monitor and navigated through the menu with the mouse. He quickly found the file that would show them the footage they would need and loaded it up. They waited patiently while the antiquated machine worked, the computer whining loudly with the effort. Eventually, the screen changed.

It was much darker than the footage they'd just seen on the screen, due to the action taking place at night and there being no streetlights in the vicinity.

The footage began at 10 p.m.

Adam checked his notes. The burner phone's battery had long since died but luckily Adam had written the details of the message on a piece of paper. The message informing Danny that his visitor had arrived had been received at 12:51 a.m., so Adam fast forwarded to 12:40 a.m.

They watched the unchanging blackness on the screen for a while, until, at 12:48 a.m., a pair of headlights passed by and headed up the road towards the hotel. It passed too quickly to get any details and even when Adam rewound the footage and paused it, the footage was too distorted to make out the make or model.

So far, so unhelpful. Adam felt his heart sink at the thought of getting so close to an answer, only for it to evaporate when it was within grabbing distance.

They waited with bated breath for the car's return.

At 12:55 a.m., it came.

This time, lady luck was on their side.

Rather than pass by at speed, it pulled into the forecourt, where it idled for a minute, thick smoke pouring out of its wide exhaust. Adam pressed pause.

The graininess of the footage meant that they could not see the driver and the make and model of the car still eluded them, though Adam was sure that that information would be discernible to a genuine petrolhead. Sadly, neither of them were that bothered by cars.

One detail that could be seen was very useful indeed.

The next little breadcrumb of the case was laid before them. Adam scribbled down the details of the number plate that was lit up for them like a neon sign.

Now, all they had to do was figure out who the car belonged to.

With some progress made, Adam unscrewed the top of his water and glugged half the bottle, not realising just how thirsty he was. He set the bottle down again and watched the screen.

They let the footage run for a few more minutes, just in case. While they watched the blackness on the screen, they discussed their next steps.

Pins and needles began to prickle in Adam's legs and as he attempted to change his position, he knocked the bottle of water over, tipping it onto the computer's keyboard.

'You dickhead,' whispered Colin, looking round the stockroom for anything they could use to mop up the spillage. He grabbed an old cloth from the sink and dabbed at the keys, hoping to soak up the moisture before it seeped into the circuitry.

Happy that no lasting damage had been done, they turned their attention back to the screen. In the watery mayhem, one of them had pressed a button that made the footage move in double time. When they looked back, the time stamp showed that the footage had moved forward by nearly an hour.

As Adam moved the mouse to close the footage, Colin grabbed his wrist. On the screen, moving slowly from the direction of the hotel, was another car without its lights on. It was easy to tell that this was not the same car, due to the shorter body.

'What a stroke of luck,' Adam said, staring with disbelief at the screen as the car crept down the road and out of sight.

'So, whoever was in the first car delivered the money to Danny and whoever was in the second car took it back by lethal force. Do you reckon that's our killer?' Colin asked.

'I'm certain of it.'

15

THE DINNER

THE STATELY HOME reminded Adam of a game of Cluedo. Whichever door you opened, there was some grandiose room behind it.

The dining room was no different.

A long table filled the middle of the large room, the antique oak so polished you could almost see yourself in it. Heavy silver cutlery flanked intricately designed plates that looked like they cost more than Adam's whole kitchen at home. An ornate chandelier bathed the room in light.

Most of the places were already taken, so Adam took a seat between Sam and Emily's father, Trevor. He nodded a greeting at the rest of the table, not wanting to interrupt conversations already in full flow.

Sam, Ross and their parents were discussing something wedding related while Emily and her bridesmaids talked about the songs they hoped the band would play tomorrow night. Emily's parents were running their fingers up and down a drinks menu, choosing which wines to buy for the impending meal.

Adam snuck a look at the prices and gulped. He sincerely hoped that the bill was on the Campbell family!

Sitting silently on the other side of the table was Mike, Emily's brother. His shirt was so fitted around his huge arms that Adam worried the blood would reach an impasse at his biceps and fail to flow to his fingers. His eyes were downcast towards the table, but his demeanour suggested he wasn't in the mood for family time. Perhaps the stress of the weekend was getting to him.

Adam wished Colin could have come, but he'd been told that the meal was strictly for the wedding party.

A waiter approached the besuited Trevor, who ordered enough bottles of wine to get an army drunk. The waiter nodded his head sagely, approving of the choices as a sommelier would, before backing slowly out of the room towards the kitchens.

Trevor adjusted his position in his seat, turning to look at Adam with all the grace of a ship's turning circle. His huge buttocks hung over the side of the seat and Adam could smell the perspiration seeping through his heavy suit jacket.

'How are you, son?' he asked.

Adam and Trevor engaged in idle chit-chat for a while, before the first course arrived. Silence fell as spoons were plucked from the table and soup was ladled into mouths. Adam took great care not to spill any on his white shirt.

When empty bowls had been collected, Emily's mother, Cynthia, got to her feet. She tapped the stem of her wine glass with a fork, bringing silence to the room once more.

'The Campbell and the McMullan families would just like to say thank you to you all for being here tonight. Weddings are stressful at the best of times, but when you consider what has happened this weekend... well...' she trailed off.

Trevor took over, hoisting his considerable frame from his seat with a loud grunt.

'What my wife is trying to say, is thank you to the young ones. You've looked after Sam and Emily under difficult circumstances, not just this weekend but in the lead up to the wedding too.'

He glanced at the empty chair at the head of the table.

'Daniel Costello was a good boy, and we were shocked and saddened by what has happened to him. I've known his father for many years. Sam, my future son-in-law, has lost his best man and a friend, as have many of you. Please, let's raise a glass in his memory.'

Everyone stood with arms extended towards the vacant chair and clinked their glasses.

The remainder of the meal passed without incident. Adam held a hand over his glass every time an offer of more wine was made. He was sure he'd never have another chance to sample a £50 bottle again, but he was determined to remain sober.

Whoever murdered Danny was going to be brought to justice tonight, he was sure of it, and for that he needed a clear head.

After the meal, the party made their way into the barroom, which was decorated in much the same manner as last night. Beige pop music was playing, though the dancefloor was empty. It felt like déjà vu to Adam, who, for a minute, had the ridiculous notion that he had been given an opportunity to intervene with fate; to stop Danny's life from ending in the way it had.

He shook his head, keen not to let his imagination run away from him. He checked his watch. Night was drawing in fast and they still had so much to do. He clocked Colin by the bar, ordering a drink.

'You best be keeping a clear head,' Adam said, sidling up to his friend.

A glass of water was passed across the bar at exactly that moment. Colin motioned to it much the same way as an assistant might highlight the star prize on a corny gameshow, before picking out the slice of lemon and throwing at Adam's face. He watched with satisfaction as it bounced off his forehead.

'We've got to leave it until people are slightly more drunk,' Adam said, moving to a table with two seats.

'What do we do until then?' Colin asked, placing his pint glass on a coaster.

'We watch.'

AN HOUR LATER, and the dancefloor was filled. Those who had arrived late to the party were well oiled, no doubt thanks to pre-drinks in bedrooms with the alcohol purchased earlier from the petrol station at the end of the road. The pop playlist had been replaced by a function band, who stormed through songs that would be repeated tomorrow night after the speeches –

whipping the crowded dancefloor into a frenzy with genuine wedding classics.

The finishing notes of *Come On, Eileen* rang out as the band downed their instruments and concluded their first set of the night, to much cheering from the appreciative horde.

As the dancefloor emptied, Adam seized his chance. He walked up to the microphone and tapped it to make sure it was on. A couple of dull thuds sounded through the PA system. The singer looked over at what he assumed was a drunken karaoke singer, but Adam held up a pacifying finger.

'A car with the number plate HFZ 4531 is blocking a staff member's car. Who does it belong to?'

This moment was not lost on Adam. Whoever held their hand up was admitting to owning the car that had stopped at the petrol station last night. The car that had just visited Danny to hand over money.

Trevor's hand shot up.

Adam left the microphone behind and walked over to him as he was pushing himself out of his seat. His eyes were unfocused and his cheeks rosy – he was certainly in no condition to drive.

'After all that wine at dinner, I'm not sure you're fit to get behind the wheel,' Adam smiled. 'I'll move it for you, Mr Campbell.'

Trevor pushed the keys into Adam's sweaty palm and patted him on the back with enough force to knock him forward a few steps.

Shaking slightly, he made his way out of the bar. Colin was waiting at reception and the two of them walked outside into the crisp air, their eyes hovering over each number plate in search for the car they needed.

Adam pressed a button on the keys, causing orange lights to blink in the encroaching darkness. They made their way to the expensive car and got in. It started with a faint purr, not like the spluttering his own rusty Clio produced upon coming to life.

He moved the car from its current position to a spot around the corner, out of sight of the windows from the bar. Here, out of the way of prying eyes, they had time to search for what they suspected might be hidden.

Adam opened the glovebox, though it was neat and orderly. Definitely nothing hidden in there. He rifled through any compartment he could, coming up empty while Colin climbed into the back of the car. He ran his hand under the mats and between the seats, again coming away empty handed.

Frustrated, he slapped the material covering the back of the passenger seat. His hand hit something solid. From the pocket, he pulled a plastic lunchbox and held it up to Adam, who stopped searching in order to appraise the find with his own eyes.

'I assume it's not food in there?' he said.

Colin ripped the plastic lid off, exposing another piece of the puzzle.

Inside was a phone. A phone that looked almost identical to the one Danny had been using as a burner.

Colin pocketed it.

'Time to find out what role Mr Campbell had in this,' he said as they exited the car.

16

THE BREAKTHROUGH

ADAM DROPPED THE keys back to Trevor, keen to make everything appear as normal as possible. The father of the bride thanked him profusely and offered to buy him a drink several times before he managed to get away. The band were back on, tearing through a Bon Jovi mega mix, and Adam was able to slip out of the room undetected.

While Adam was busy in the bar, Colin took it upon himself to partake in a little side mission. Instead of going back to their bedroom when he bid his friend goodbye, he carried on walking down the corridor towards the room Danny had previously occupied.

His first visit to the room had been necessary. The second visit had been risky, and he'd almost been caught snooping around by the authorities. Going back for a third time was surely madness. But the beginnings of a plan had formed upon leaving Trevor's car, and the plan was dependent on retrieving something from the stricken best man's room.

If he got caught, he could just act drunk and plead ignorance. He'd simply opened the door to the wrong room. And if anything, it was the staff's fault for leaving the door unlocked in the first place.

He crept down the corridor slowly, praying that the door *had* indeed been left unlocked by the staff who had other things on their minds. When he reached his destination, he cast a glance around before trying the handle. It seemed someone had been listening to his hasty prayer…

Adam and Colin arrived back at the room at roughly the same time. Adam shot his friend a quizzical look, though Colin shook his head.

Not here.

Adam opened the door to their bedroom and they entered, keen to uncover whatever evidence was stored on the phone.

Colin could feel the surge of adrenaline as the phone came slowly to life; the dim screen displaying a welcome message. He could see his friend's hand was shaking.

Adam was nervous. If Trevor *was* involved in this, it would be a major scandal on the North Coast. His business was worth more money than Adam could imagine, and it would be Adam's name forever attached to bringing it down. Also, the guy was the size of a house and built like a brick...

'Shall we see what it says?' Colin asked, noticing Adam's sudden reticence.

Adam shook himself from the image of Trevor standing over him with the veins bulging in his slab of a forehead. The call list was empty, as expected. Presumably, this phone was the only means of communication between Danny and Trevor. Danny would never have had the balls to blackmail someone by talking on the phone to them. Instead, he'd have relied on text messages – it was so much easier to say cowardly things with written words.

The presumption turned out to be correct.

Trevor was not as technologically savvy as Danny and had not thought to delete any of the messages he'd received or sent. Adam and Colin spent ten minutes taking in every detail of the correspondence, looking on with disbelieving eyes.

'Jesus,' Adam said, setting the phone down and letting the information permeate. Colin sat back in his chair and did the same. Neither spoke for a few minutes.

'So,' Colin said, eventually. 'Danny saw Sam and some random girl kiss on the stag do. He then got in contact with Mr Campbell to tell him that unless he paid Danny to keep the information to himself, he might accidently let that information slip to Emily who would be devastated.'

'£50 to start with, which Trevor probably thought was a one-off payment and worth it to stop a load of hassle. No wonder Sam said things have been tense between Trevor and him – imagine your future father-in-law knew you'd been unfaithful and was paying to cover it up!'

'So, he paid the money but then got another text from Danny a week later saying that he was feeling loose lipped and that he'd need another £50 to guarantee that his lips remained sealed. Then, no further correspondence until yesterday when he received another message asking for more.'

'Which he paid just after midnight. Then, an hour or so later, Danny was dead.'

'So, who is his accomplice?'

'If there is an accomplice,' Adam said. 'For all we know, Trevor has had no part in this, aside from being the victim.'

This was all becoming too much of a mind wrecker. Colin wished they'd never got involved.

'We don't know who the killer is or how they managed to persuade Danny to take tablets he was allergic to. We're no closer to solving this, and unless you fancy marching up to Trevor and asking if he is our murderer, which would be utterly ridiculous, there's no way forward.' Colin let out a long sigh. 'I need a drink. Where's your hipflask?'

Those three words hit Adam like a ton of lead.

The hipflask.

'When you searched Danny's room, did you see a hipflask that looked identical to mine?'

Colin wracked his brain but couldn't remember seeing it. He shook his head.

'I think I know who did it,' Adam said, moving to the door.

COLIN FOLLOWED ADAM down the hallway. The low rumble of the bassline and the thump of the drums drifted through the closed doors, telling them that the band were still keeping people's attention in the confines of the bar. Adam hoped that the person whose room they were about to visit was either on the dancefloor or sitting happily at a table, tapping his foot and not waiting for them behind the door.

A boy Adam recognised from school – and a girl he did not – sauntered past them, hand in hand, presumably towards one of their rooms. Adam felt a pang of annoyance. He should be enjoying the party and attempting to reap the rewards of being on the wedding party by trying to crack on with one of the bridesmaids. Instead, here he was, putting himself in harm's way to try to solve the murder of someone he didn't even *really* like.

When they reached the door they needed, Adam tried the handle, but it didn't budge. Thankfully, the room was around a corner from the main hallway and afforded them some privacy. Colin kept lookout while Adam attempted to work his magic on the lock.

For several minutes, he waggled a paperclip in the lock and was thankful to both YouTube and the ancient, basic locking system within the door when he felt it give. The door creaked open slowly.

Adam's heart raced at the thought of walking into the lion's den, but everything that this tiring day had thrown at them had led them here. He was now so close to discovering if his hunch was correct or not, and that fuelled his steps across the threshold and into the room.

Colin continued to keep watch while Adam searched the room. Aside from an open case on the floor and a few ripples on the bedcovers, one might assume the room was unused. Certainly, the keeper of the keys hadn't spent much time in here aside from getting ready for the evening's festivities.

Adam took a quick look in the obvious places but came away empty handed. He cast an eye around the room and settled on the case. Surely, if you had something to hide, it'd be in there.

He poked at some clothes, moving them out of the way while trying to keep everything as it was. As the seconds ticked by, his searching became more erratic. He tipped everything out and patted items down before moving them to the side.

'Hurry up,' Colin hissed.

'I'm going as fast as I can,' Adam whispered back.

Suddenly, something caught his eye. A colour that tugged at a memory. He grabbed the trousers and thrust his hand in the pocket, pulling out a wad of cash. He had no time to count it now, but he'd bet it totalled £200.

Sure that the hipflask was not amongst the clothes, he began scooping trousers and T-shirts up and was about to pile them back in the case when his eyes happened upon something.

In the case, sewn into the lining, was a zip. It was the same colour as the fabric and could be easily missed.

Adam pulled it slowly. In the silence, the noise of the material sounded like bison charging across a desert plain, such was the volume of the material parting.

Colin's head appeared around the doorway.

'There are footsteps on the stairs,' he whispered. 'I think someone is coming.'

Quickly, Adam reached into the compartment, his fingers knocking against something cold and hard.

His heart leapt.

He pulled the hipflask out of its hiding place and showed it to Colin. The engraved initials, D.C., twinkled in the light of the room. He reached in again and grabbed the other item – a key.

'Great,' Colin said. 'Now, let's go.'

Adam stood and watched as his friend peeked around the corner of the wall. Whoever had been ascending the stairs had obviously gone into another room along the corridor as the hallway was empty.

'Ready?' Colin asked.

Adam nodded and they both sprinted along the corridor, not stopping until they reached their room.

'WE'RE SURE IT'S him?' Colin asked when the adrenaline had once again subsided.

Adam shrugged. He looked at the pile of money, which totalled just over £300.

'The money doesn't necessarily point the finger of guilt his way. It's more than Danny had asked for. But I reckon it, coupled with the hipflask, do. Why else would he have it?'

Colin agreed, though took another few minutes to cast a spotlight over the evidence they'd uncovered, just in case they'd missed anything. He couldn't see that they had.

'How do we go about confronting him though?' Adam said.

Colin smiled at him. To his mind, it had felt like Adam had been the leader all day. Now, he had an idea. He went to his jacket and from it pulled out the item he had taken from Danny's room less than an hour ago.

Adam shot him a confused look.

'It's the phone charger for Danny's burner. I thought rather than us storming in and pointing fingers, we'd let our accused do the admitting. It's how it's usually done on TV dramas – you trick them into spilling the beans.'

'And I assume you have a plan?' Adam asked.

'That I do,' Colin answered.

17

A MEETING IN THE MOONLIGHT

ADAM TYPED A message on Danny's now charged burner. He kept it short and sweet and when he was happy, pressed send. Instantly, an alert appeared on Trevor's phone, telling him that a message had been received.

Part one of the plan was in place.

As he set the phone down on the table, a strange longing took him. Sure, he loved his modern smartphone with the world at his fingertips, but there was something brilliant about a phone that you could still play *Snake* on and only needed to be charged once a week.

While Adam was taking care with that side of the plan, Colin dealt with the other. When he was finished, he nodded at his friend.

'Twenty minutes or so,' he said.

Adam let out a long sigh. He was jittery, and his foot was tapping a rhythm on the carpet with such ferocity that it sounded like a death metal blast beat. Colin knew how he felt. The plan was in place, the adrenaline was flowing and all they could do was wait.

Time ticked by slowly. After ten minutes that felt like a lifetime, Adam stood.

'I can't stand it anymore,' he said. 'By the time we put phase one into motion, phase two will be ready.'

'Five more minutes,' Colin answered. 'We don't want to rush in and be out of our depth.'

'Three minutes,' Adam countered, and Colin ceded defeat with a quick nod.

Colin looked at the time on his watch. If this evenings' entertainment was following last night's timescale, the music would be stopping in about ten minutes and the bar would be emptying out. If they were to be successful, they needed to get in and out of the bar as if partaking in a military operation.

They walked down the stairs, noticing more people in the foyer than anticipated. Perhaps the band were finishing early. Adam swore under his breath and picked up the pace, crossing the wooden floor in double time.

To their relief, the function room was still crowded. The band were storming through a rousing rendition of Dancing Queen and everyone on the dancefloor was showing their appreciation by singing along loudly.

Colin spotted their target in the middle of a dance circle with his back to them. He felt Adam tap him on the arm. He looked at where his friend was pointing – at one of the tables near the back of the room. The lights from the band's rig lit up the table at random intervals, allowing Colin to see a fashionable jacket draped over the back of a chair.

'Is that his?' he asked.

Adam confirmed it was.

Colin took a deep breath. If he was seen by the owner of the jacket, the plan would burst into flames. Before his courage could desert him, he took a step in the direction of the jacket, picking up the pace as he crossed the carpeted floor.

When he reached the table, he thrust Trevor's mobile phone into a pocket of the velvety jacket and moved away from it as quickly as he could, as if it were about to blow up.

He retraced his steps back to the edge of the dancefloor, keeping out of the light as best he could. He cast covert glances at the owner of the jacket and was pretty sure he hadn't been spotted. As he and Adam slipped out of the door, the band announced that they only had one song left.

So far, things were going to plan.

ADAM CHECKED HIS watch again. Twenty minutes had passed and nothing had happened. He wondered if the ambitious plan had been thwarted.

'What do we do?' he said.

Colin shrugged.

'Nothing's changed,' he said. 'He'll be here.'

Though his words were firm, his tone was not. Adam could hear the doubt in his voice, but, having no plan B, they did all they could do – wait.

Colin looked out of the large window of the marquee. It framed the full moon that hung in the inky, cloudless sky, illuminating the sprawling lawn outside.

It was like something from a fairy tale and he would've normally savoured such a picturesque scene, were it not for the fact they were waiting for a killer to appear in their midst.

Suddenly, a shadow appeared on the grass outside, growing longer by the second. A minute later, the fabric doors at the rear of the marquee flapped open and there he stood, bathed in the warm light of the moon.

'You two?' he said, noticing Adam and Colin at the front of the domed tent. 'You're the blackmailers?'

'Not really,' said Adam. 'Sorry, Mike, but we needed to make you think that to get you to come here. You see, we've figured out that it was you who killed Danny.'

'Very clever,' said Mike, holding up his father's burner phone. 'You used dead Danny's phone to send another blackmailing message to my father and put it in my pocket, knowing I'd see it and rise to it. Well, A+ for creativity.'

Adam snorted. The shy, retiring Michael Campbell of a few years ago would never have used such a corny line. But it seemed it wasn't only his appearance that had undergone a makeover.

'How did you figure out it was me then?' he asked.

Adam wished that they weren't so far away from each other. It made sense to stay away, of course; he was a murderer after all, but Adam's throat was beginning to hurt from having spoken so much today. And now he was expected to communicate from such a distance. He considered ringing the burner in Mike's hand, but thought it a bit over the top. Colin would never let him live it down.

'Well,' he said. 'we don't know everything, so we're hoping you can help us fill in a few blanks.'

Mike said nothing, so Adam continued.

'We knew Danny was blackmailing somebody on account of him having met with someone who gave him an envelope full of cash. We just didn't know who had given it to him. Luckily, a kindly lady at the petrol station down the road let us look at her CCTV footage. We saw your dad's car park up not long after Danny took receipt of the money.'

He cleared his throat, longing for a soothing mouthful of Lemsip.

'We knew your dad couldn't have killed him because we saw him drive away, though we suspect he's involved in some way. But another car came past a while later. Your car, I assume.'

Mike nodded.

'You see, when I saw you at the party, you weren't drunk at all. You made a scene to make it *look* like you were drunk. How could someone who was falling over themself drive a car? It was clever, I'll give you that.'

'I was hoping to remain unseen,' Mike said. 'When you bumped into me, I had to come up with something on the spot.'

'It was convincing,' admitted Adam. 'And it definitely threw us off the scent.'

'So, what put you back on it?'

'Colin found the tablet package you left in Danny's bin. Everyone knows he is allergic, so would have had no reason to have them. That's when we knew it was definitely murder. Then, we broke into your room and found his room key that you stole from Ross's jacket and Danny's hipflask. We just don't know how you actually got him to take the tablets.'

'Very clever,' Mike said, taking a seat in the back row. 'Shall I tell you my side of things?'

He took a steadying breath.

'After I got back from the stag do, dad was miserable. I didn't know why, but he was angry with everyone, even Emily. That's when I knew things were bad. Then, one day, I saw him with this old Nokia. He left it lying about and I saw the messages, I knew what Danny was up to.'

'Does your dad know that you know?'

'No,' he said. 'He has no idea. He would've kept paying to keep Sam's disgusting secret from his darling daughter Emily forevermore.'

'So, you took matters into your own hands?'

'I was hoping to remain unseen last night. When you saw me, I was looking for Danny to have a chat to try to persuade him to ease off. I saw Sam and him have a fight and watched him storm off. I was going to follow him then, but I needed him in a more receptive mood, so I waited. Later, I saw Sam come back from Danny's room and give Ross a key. I assumed it was for his room so I stole it when Ross was dancing.'

'And you paid Danny a visit?'

'I did. I went to his room. He was on his way out and, when he saw me, started to brag about controlling dad like a puppet. He wouldn't listen to what I had to say, so I walked around the corner and waited for him to leave. When I knew he was gone, I went back and popped some dissolving tablets into the hipflask. And then I waited for him to come back. As soon as he came in, I punched him, got him on the bed and held his mouth open while I poured a cocktail of whiskey and paracetamol down his throat. He tried to resist, but it didn't take long for his airways to close up and he died pretty quickly.'

Colin was astonished at how casual Mike had told his story – like he was telling them about a nice bike ride he'd been on.

'How did you know he was allergic?' he asked.

Mike snorted.

'Because he wouldn't stop going on about it on the stag do. He made it seem as if suffering through a hangover without painkillers was the same as being crucified. So, I pocketed that information to be used at a later date.'

'But why?' Colin asked, rage seeping into his words.

'Why?' Mike asked as he pushed himself to standing. 'Because him and Sam were the reason school was hell for me.

They were the reason everyone else thought it was OK to pick on me or throw my lunch on the roof or…'

He trails off for a minute, before composing himself.

'And then, to find out Sam McMullan is marrying into my family was the last straw. Everyone knew Danny was a dick, but no one knew how awful Sam could be. I knew I had to find a way to get the wedding cancelled.'

'Why not just tell your sister about Sam kissing the girl on his stag?'

'Because I didn't want to hurt her, directly. Yes, I know she's dad's favourite and all, but we're close. She didn't deserve such blunt honesty.'

'So, you killed a man instead, in the hope that that would force the wedding to be called off?'

'Honestly,' he said. 'I didn't mean to kill him. I thought maybe he'd have a massive reaction, and we'd call the ambulance, and he'd be fine but Sam wouldn't have been able to go through with the wedding or something. But, hearing him brag about taking money from my family and watching him swan around like he owned the place, well… it changed my mind. The world is a better place without Daniel Costello.'

With his spiel finished, silence filled the marquee.

'So, what next?' Mike asked.

'What's next is that you are under arrest for the murder of Daniel Costello,' said a gruff voice from the door.

Adam and Colin watched as the small team of police officers slid from their hiding places and swarmed Mike, taking him to the ground before slipping cuffs over his wrists. One of the officers read him his rights as he was dragged into a standing position by the others.

Mike cast a pleading glance back at Adam and Colin as he was led out of the marquee towards the waiting unmarked police car at the end of the gardens.

Adam and Colin collapsed into their seats; the fatigue of a long, punishing day washing over them. Adam took the hipflask from his pocket and unscrewed the lid before taking a huge slug. He passed it to his friend.

'I'll tell you what,' Colin said, between mouthfuls. 'The old folk at work are going to love hearing about this.'

18

A GROWING REPUTATION

THREE WEEKS LATER

ADAM FLICKED HIS hair to one side, before changing his mind and sweeping it to the other. He looked in the mirror on the underside of the sun visor to make sure he'd made the correct decision before turning to Colin, who was in the back seat.

'Ready for a big night out?' he asked.

Colin flashed him a smile. The local nightclub, Atmosphere, always promised fun. The only tragic thing was, they were being driven there by Adam's mum, who had insisted that paying over the odds for a taxi was stupid.

'It's a shame Sam and Emily decided to cancel the wedding,' she said. 'But, if there's infidelity at the start, it's not a good foundation to build a marriage on. Sam has a bit of growing up to do.'

She looked at her son, who was drumming along to some abrasive metal song. When she'd heard what he had gotten up to on the weekend of the wedding, he had gone up a notch in her estimations. She smiled as she pulled into a space a few hundred metres away from the club, knowing they'd be mortified if she dropped them right outside the door.

To her surprise, Adam leant across and planted a sloppy kiss on her cheek. She assumed it was because of the several beers he'd had in his room with Colin before they'd left, but she appreciated the sentiment, anyway.

'Be safe,' she said as he slipped out of the door. Colin waved at her as they crossed the road.

Adam and Colin stood at the bar, neither of them quite drunk enough to dance yet. They were jostled side to side as they attempted to order a round of drinks, eventually managing to do so. Beers in hand, they walked through an archway into a quieter part of the club.

They took a seat and talked about anything and everything for a while. After a few more beers, Adam felt the alcohol start to take hold of him. He could feel his thoughts drift and his speech slur.

Colin watched his friend's eyes start to squint slightly as the volume of his words increased.

What a lightweight, he thought.

Their conversation was interrupted by a high-pitched squeal. They looked round to find Zoe, one of Emily's bridesmaids, on her hands and knees, having tripped over the leg of a chair. Her friends were laughing so much they weren't even bothering to help, instead filming her squirm helplessly on the floor on their smartphones.

Adam jumped out of his chair and extended a helping hand. Zoe looked up and beamed at him, recognition spreading across her face.

'Do you just go around rescuing everyone who is in need?' she asked, touching his chest.

Adam tried to ignore the light touch on his chest and attempted to say something witty, causing Colin to cringe at what actually came out. Zoe didn't seem to notice, and if she did, she didn't care.

'I thought what you did at the wedding was very brave,' she said, grabbing his hand. 'Do you want to dance with me?'

Adam looked at Colin with wide eyes.

Colin nodded at him, as if encouraging a child to take its first steps. He watched as Zoe led Adam away. Her friends, who had laughed at her misfortune, sat down at a nearby table. Colin vaguely recognised them from the wedding weekend. One of them glanced across.

'I recognise you from the papers,' she said. 'Didn't you help solve the murder too?'

Colin nodded, getting up from his seat and moving to their table.

'I was the brains behind the whole thing,' he said.

ABOUT THE AUTHOR

Originally hailing from the north coast of Northern Ireland and now residing in South Manchester, Chris McDonald has always been a reader. At primary school, The Hardy Boys inspired his love of adventure, before his reading world was opened up by Chuck Palahniuk and the gritty world of crime. He's a fan of 5-a-side football, has an eclectic taste in music ranging from Damien Rice to Slayer and loves dogs.

Printed in Great Britain
by Amazon